The Rhoberts Brothers

By

Kevin P. Ellis

PublishAmerica
Baltimore

ISBN: 1-4241-4421-3
PUBLISHED BY PUBLISHAMERICA, LLLP
www.publishamerica.com
Baltimore

Printed in the United States of America

This book is dedicated to God and family.
My family would include, but is not limited to
Ellis, Griffin, Fowell, Norrid, Marcum, Hamiter, Noel, Smith, Heyse,
Raines, Thatcher, Clifton, Flores, Schwab, Till and Fuentes.
(Not in any specific order)
Without them, this book would have been written a lot sooner.

Chapter 1

"Remember, look, listen, feel, taste and smell. Listen to your gut. Stay focused. Too much ginseng in my green tea. You're on the clock, genius. Head in the game...Head in the game...I saw nothing; it's too damn dark...I heard the sirens reflecting off of those dark, empty warehouses. The sirens are close. Someone must have called about the quick car chase. I don't like it. I felt the breeze on my mask. There was no taste; there was no smell. You have to love the heat and humidity around here. It caused my underwear to get sweaty. I absolutely hated when that happens. I'll take it out on the target," thought Kyle.

About five minutes ago, Kyle Rhoberts started following a vehicle that matched a description he had been given. He ran the license plate of the vehicle through their computer. The plate was reported stolen in a car jacking (along with the vehicle). Kyle knew this particular story because it happened only three hours ago. The female victim, or driver if you will, was shot in the back. The victims's two children jumped out of the vehicle on their own.

"Good for them. Most kids would freeze or would go in to shock. (Curious?) They probably got out when their mother was shot. Whether it was fear for themselves, or fear for their mother, who knows? Self-preservation? Selfish preservation? Is there a difference? Who cares why they got out? Hope they didn't abandon mom to save their own skin. It will haunt them later if they did. Wait a minute; they were kids for God's sake. DAMN IT! I'm ranting again. Head in the game…Head in the game…" thought Kyle.

The vehicle, or suspected target, sped off after he noticed Kyle in his rear view mirror. "Who can effectively trail someone when it's 3:00 A.M. and there are about twenty cars moving on this side of town? Not me," thought Kyle. "Oh well." Shortly after noticing Kyle in his rear view mirror, his excessive speed in a turn caused him to spin out and lose control in the gravel of the right shoulder. He popped both rear tires in the spin. His facial expressions in the turns were hilarious. His eyes were wide open, and he had a surprised expression on his face. He panicked; "I love it when they do that," thought Kyle. "Adrenaline was too much for him. Probably soiled himself. Hey, that's funny too." He jumped out of the vehicle and took off running towards the warehouse district of northwest Dallas. That means Kyle was on foot too. "From the glimpse I got, he appeared to be a white male, twenty years old, six foot, and about 200 pounds."

"Target acquired," said Kyle in to his microphone. The target had a shaved head with blonde stubble. "What's with the shaved heads lately?" asked Kyle to himself. He was also wearing the inevitable blue jeans and a white t-shirt. That matched the target description to a tee. "Excellent!" Time was ticking for Cue-ball. The sirens were getting louder. Kyle had about three minutes before it rained blue. Typically, a slow, methodical search of these warehouses would be necessary for someone else. Not Kyle. He knew exactly where Cue-ball was.

His name was Kenny Rhoberts. He worked inside an apartment building that had been closed and fenced off for years. The grounds all around the complex had been dried out and cracked since he bought it. There wasn't a blade of grass on the entire property. There wasn't a single window left intact and Kenny and Kyle had unwanted pets everywhere. (Rats for the most part.) The roof had caved in, and fallen porches, stairwells and covered parking tops helped to define this as a unique antique. At least, that was what the realtor had posted. By the way, the genius that was standing out in the open in the warehouse district was Kenny's brother Kyle. Kyle was probably standing there, thinking of a movie quote, or calling someone a badass bum. (BAB for short.) He thought too much and pondered on things that boggled the mind.

To give you an example, Kyle and Kenny were movie buffs. Kenny enjoyed reading novels as well, but Kyle was strictly a movie man. Kenny and Kyle were watching an older movie about the Book of Genesis. Kyle wanted to know why they never showed you the navels of Adam and Eve. He believed that since they were the first, they could not possibly have had them. However, to be without would look too weird. This was what Kenny dealt with on a daily basis. Kyle thought that the director wasn't sure about the navels, so they blurred the mid section on purpose to keep you guessing. Kenny was bothered by the entire conversation and would leave to go surf the web. Was Kenny ranting now as well? Too bad. Anyway, back to the warehouse district.

Kyle was wearing a set of specially designed goggles underneath a SWAT mask. Kenny designed them. The mask was black, lightweight, and breathed easy. The mask didn't get wet near the mouth because of Kyle's excessive breathing or bantering. The cloth covering the mouth area was very thin and porous. It allowed Kyle to breathe easy and it filtered some basic compounds from the air. The goggles were connected to a tiny computer that Kyle carried on his back. The computer was state of the art and had many functions. It enabled the goggles to change with a simple command. For night vision, Kenny would type in the word, "night." For infrared body heat detection, Kenny would type in the words, "body heat." For Kyle's prescription lenses, Kenny would type in the word, "bat" (as in *blind as a*), and so on. There were more functions, but you will learn those later.

Kyle carried a modified KR-7. It was a fully automatic assault weapon with silencer. In case you didn't notice, the KR-7 was Kenny's creation, and his initials. It carried a .357 round and held as many as Kyle deemed necessary, which he was going to need very shortly, in Kenny's opinion. Kyle had a microphone on his uniform and could activate it when he wanted. He normally liked the mic a lot. Kenny and Kyle opted not to have it on at all times because feedback noise was a possibility. Kenny built in a LED screen on the bottom of the goggles for quick messages. He was sending him a message now. The LED from Kenny read, "2½ minutes, genius!"

Kyle activated the mike and gave the appropriate response, "Eat it, Harvey! Moving in."

"Kenny worried too much in that damn apartment. Looking at all those computer screens and listening to the police band, it's dulling his mind. It's amazing he's sane. Ole Kenny boy needs some rest and relaxation. Maybe we will take a break after this one. Or not. Ah ha! Cue-ball's on the move. Body heat signature showing him moving towards the back of warehouse six. I can beat him to the back if I move it," thought Kyle.

Another LED message from Kenny, "2 minutes until the ball drops." Kyle was running, trying to keep the noise down to a minimum. He was also trying not to bust his butt. Kyle was forced to open a lens on the goggles to show the ground and any obstacles that did not generate heat. "I'm closing in on the back door. SHIT! I lost him," whispered Kyle while he opened his mike. "Cue-ball?" asked Kyle.

LED response from Kenny was, "I lost him too, could be one of the old iron work warehouses, want to abort?"

Kyle's opened his mike, "Negative, moving in." There was no time to wait. Kyle stayed on the hinge side of the door. The hinges were on the outside. "This contractor wasn't very smart," thought Kyle. "Lucky for us, though." Kyle took out a small sample of gun oil and smeared it in excess on the hinges, just in case. And yes, Kyle did keep a small sample of gun oil in his tactical vest. Kyle's goggles turned to night vision. "Excellent job, brother," thought Kyle, though he would never say it aloud.

The door opened from left to right. Kyle moved to the left side of the door at the handle end. He turned the handle and it opened. "Beauty! I'll have to do this quick," thought Kyle. His left hand threw the door open. Dust particles were in the air; looked like fireflies. Kyle entered the warehouse walking fast, his footsteps echoing throughout the warehouse. "Keep the knees bent, scanning left to right, while leaning forward," thought Kyle. A quick flash of light on Kyle's left side. Muzzle fire! "Damn! He's quick. Cannot breathe well, and don't know why. Later!" Kyle turned to face target Cue-ball, and his goggles switched from night vision to his prescription sunglasses? "What the hell is he doing?" asked Kyle to himself in a panic. The large fluorescent lights in the warehouse had burst on. Talk about being enlightened. Kyle saw him in the northwest corner covering his eyes from the light. Kyle sent a small burst into Cue-ball's chest. Down he went. Kyle was starting to breathe easier. He must have taken one of Cue's rounds in the vest.

"Lucky shot," thought Kyle. Cue-ball threw the gun away from himself. "If this is an attempt at mercy, you are sadly mistaken, my murderous friend," thought Kyle while he walked over towards him. Kyle could hear the spent shells clinking against each other inside the insulated box attached to the ejection port. They caught the empty .357 rounds that he fired. "No evidence. Have to bring that up to Kenny," and Kyle opened his mike, "BAB, did you get the picture?" asked Kyle.

LED response, "Got it, killing the lights and you have got 30 seconds," said Kenny. Kyle's burst hit him square in the chest. "He won't make it. Good," thought Kyle.

"Help me," Cue-ball whispered.

"No women, no kids," replied Kyle as he raised the weapon, switched it to semi-automatic and shot one round in his head. Lights went out, goggles to night vision and Kyle was out the back door and down an embankment into a small creek that led out of the warehouse district.

LED response from Kenny read, "The movie is *The Professional*, and don't get the gun wet."

Kyle opened his mike, "Too late, BAB."

Chapter 2

Patrol officers got there first, as usual. Took them a while, but they found the power switch and turned on the lights in warehouse six. Standard procedure followed and they marked off the area with yellow crime scene tape. Kenny and Kyle were waiting for detectives and crime scene personnel to make their appearances. "Probably called an ambulance so they could officially declare Cue-ball deceased. Why can't cops do that? Does it take a genius to take a pulse? Check for breathing?" thought Kenny. The suits came in.

"There's our buddy, Detective Jesse James," said Kyle to his brother Kenny. (They called him Jesse-Boy.) Why would his parents torture him like that? Bet he played a lot of cops and robbers. Was he cop or robber? Also bet he got his butt beat at the playground a lot. Detective James knew the Rhobertses' work. He had been on their tail for the last six months. He was about five foot ten and 200 pounds. He was Caucasian with brown hair and brown eyes. His taste in suits was decent, but the ties were horrendous. Five-hundred-dollar suits and a twenty-dollar tie. He was wearing the piano keys necktie today. "I really hate ties, especially that one," thought Kenny. "I'll have to add it to my list of hate-age." He seemed to be living up to the name.

You see, Jesse-Boy always found himself in conflict at those crime scenes. On one hand, you had another dead bad guy and another story that hit the press about another bad guy dying. Those stories had a profound effect on the crime statistics lately. They had obviously shown a decrease in crime all over Dallas. Now, on the other hand, Jesse-Boy did take his job seriously, and he did not care for the idea of a vigilante running loose on his streets. It appeared that most of the patrol officers liked the job they were doing. The Rhobertses were guessing it was less work for Patrol, and they would not have many repeat offenders.

Detective James had already found the Rhobertses' camera. Kenny made the smallest camera you have ever seen. It looked like a kid's marble. Once separated from the battery pack, it had a life span of about twenty minutes. Jesse-Boy always found the marble and put it in his briefcase. Bet he gave them to the local boys club. It was getting boring there anyway. It had started to look like a Krispy Kreme grand opening. (The chocolate eclairs are sinful.)

Crime scene analyst Drew Michaels had the gift. In the academy, they said that Michaels could find a needle in a haystack. And he could. That was ten years ago. Michaels did a short stint in Patrol, like everyone else. but wanted crime scene more than anything. Some have the gift, and some do not. Drew had it, and he was the best crime scene analyst Detective James had ever seen. Drew Michaels was of African American descent and from his appearance, worked out a lot. He had straight, shoulder-length hair and was light complected, about five foot seven and 180 pounds. (He was a mutt, just like all Americans.) Michaels called over to Detective James. "We found a bullet, Detective," said Michaels.

"Let me guess, .357 magnum, special order," replied James.

"Yeah, I think it's your guy! But I won't be sure until I check ballistics," said Michaels.

Detective James bent down to get a closer look at the deceased. "Do it! And it's at least two guys, not one."

Michaels was confused. Same gun, same bullets. Same method of operation, or M.O., and disappeared like a ghost. "How can it be two guys?" asked Michaels.

Detective James had put on his Armani jacket and grabbed his briefcase. He turned to Michaels on his way out and said, "It's real simple. Ask yourself these questions, this many signal 27's (dead bodies) and no word on the streets whatsoever? Why was no one talking? Why did they only nail what appeared to be repeat offenders? If a patrol officer heard the shot, the suspect was always gone before anyone ever saw him. How was that? We always found some kind of evidence that proved the suspect moved away from the officer's advance. Is it luck? No." Detective James walked further out, turned back to Michaels and said, "One to pull the trigger, and one to lead the way out."

Chapter 3

"How did we do?" asked Kyle as he entered the apartment.

"We did well. I already sent the photo to John Doe, and payment has been delivered," replied Kenny.

"You got to love John Doe. I know I do," said Kyle.

"You love all men, homo," said Kenny.

"Shut up, sword-swallowing, carnival freak," replied Kyle.

Kenny laughed and said, "Dad said you were adopted, but I think Mom got you at the pound." Kyle smirked at Kenny and gave no response.

"So any new assignments?" asked Kyle.

"None tonight, I told John that we were off for a couple of days," replied Kenny.

"Good, I'm going to bed," said Kyle.

"Well…Bye," quoted Kenny.

Kyle turned around and replied, "*Tombstone*, and don't waste my time." While Kyle was replying to Kenny, he noticed Kenny's computer screen turning red. Kyle motioned to Kenny's computer and asked, "What's that all about?"

Kenny replied, "Suit up, bro, we have uninvited guests!"

Kyle came back in the room after approximately thirty-eight seconds with most of his gear attached, and with Kenny's gear in hand. "Where are the bunnies?" asked Kyle as he passed Kenny his gear.

"Two of them are getting closer to the pit," replied Kenny.

"This is gonna be a good show," said Kyle. "Wait a minute, two of them? How many are there?" asked Kyle.

"Eight," Kenny replied.

"Eight? Is that all they are sending these days?" Kyle asked.

"Maybe these guys are good," Kenny said. He no more than finished his sentence, and the air horns had sounded in the pit.

Kyle started laughing, and said, "Can't be that good; those two fell in the pit." The main reason Kyle was ecstatic with laughter, was that he invented the pit. Every time someone landed in it, he became overwhelmed with pride. "Are these friendlies or trainees? Do we know yet?" asked Kyle.

"They're friendlies, you doober; can't you see the colonel?" asked Kenny. Kenny told Kyle that maybe he was still wired from the action earlier, and Kyle told him off in not so nice of a way. Kyle said he would not miss this show for the world.

Going back to the pit, Kyle wanted to make his own contributions to the obstacle course that the Rhobertses had laid out in the apartment complex. It was a welcome to all of their guests, whether they were invited or uninvited. The invited men belonged to a friend of the Rhoberts brothers' father. His name was Colonel Sheldon Smith, and he trained Special Forces to elude capture and detection. Or he attempted to, anyway. The brothers loved this part the most. Training rookies. Kenny had set the computer on intruder alert to activate all booby traps and headed for the field.

The brothers had a series of tunnels running under the complex. They were crude because they made them themselves. The tunnels had lights because Kyle does not see well in the dark. Kyle took the back tunnel to sneak up behind them. Kenny waited up at the front of the complex. No doubt, the colonel would want to lead them to the

Rhobertses' base of operations. Not because that was the objective, but because he could take a break with the Rhobertses when they finished off his team. This was not a cakewalk or weekend at a survival camp. This was one of the final exams that some of the Special Forces trainees went through to graduate, and it's no holds barred.

Chapter 4

"Team leader to blue team, advance on the highest active power source at location alpha 1."

"What kind of op puts you in the middle of an abandoned apartment complex of a major U.S. city? Whose team were we here to find and neutralize? The colonel was not very specific on this one." Fuentes guessed that was the point. "We don't always get loads of intel," thought Sergeant Fuentes of Special Forces. Air horns had sounded, "Blue team, report status," said Fuentes.

"Blue two, OK!"

"Blue three, OK!"

"Blue four, OK?"

"Blue five, OK, but we lost blue six and seven to some kind of hole in the ground camouflaged as a filled-in swimming pool!"

"Team leader, per the colonel's instructions, consider blue six and seven neutralized, continue to advance but watch your footing." Fuentes knew six and seven would screw this up. Glory hounds that looked for the quick win. Served them right. He would remember to give them extra PT when they got back to base. "Tatatatatat" (fire from behind).

"Blue team, converge on the fire," said Fuentes.

"Blue leader, this is three, taking fire from unknown at delta 5 sector."

"Blue leader this is four, I've been hit."

"Blue leader to four, in a red area? Over."

"Affirmative, blue leader," said four.

"Blue leader to four, you're out." Red areas were killing zone areas of the body. Extremities were yellow. A yellow hit and you were still in the game. Two yellows and you were out. One red hit and you were out. "Blue leader to three, are you still taking fire?"

"..."

"Blue leader to three, are you still engaged?"

"Five to blue leader."

"Go five!"

"Blue three is tied to a pole, weapon missing and..."

"Blue leader to five, and what, five?"

While chuckling, "Five to blue leader, three has a baby pacifier taped to his mouth."

"Five, leave three to ponder his mistakes, and proceed to alpha 1. Over."

Still laughing, "Received, blue leader, five out."

"Only three of us left and I'll bet the colonel isn't happy," thought Fuentes.

"Two to blue leader."

"Blue leader to two, go ahead."

"I have reached alpha 1 structure; orders?"

"Two, stand by for back-up; confirm order. Over."

"Received, blue leader; standing by."

"If two made it to alpha 1, I'll follow his path," thought Fuentes.

"Blue leader to five, distance from alpha 1?"

"Five to blue leader, converging on two now."

"Blue leader to two and five, move in on alpha 1 structure while leader takes the Charlie side; move now, now, now." Blue two swung open the door to find total darkness inside the room. There was a quick, low, muffled sound and two and five went down writhing in pain. "Blue leader to two and five, give me your status. Over." No response. "Blue leader to team, I am converging on two and five's location."

"Blue one to leader, that is not advisable, blue leader," said an observing Colonel Smith.

"Let me run my team, Colonel. Blue leader out," said Fuentes. Blue leader reached the alpha side to observe two and five trying to pull out the taser hooks still embedded in their necks. Another five-second jolt sent two and five in to their impressions of fish out of water. While watching this and trying to ascertain an entry into the alpha structure, Kyle put two red paint balls on blue leader's chest.

"Blue one to all team members, this exercise is over. Blue leader, take your team and assemble back at the insertion point. Oh yeah, get six and seven out of the pit and someone untie three."

Kyle approached Blue leader and said, "You guys actually got farther than most; not bad, kid."

Kenny came out of the dark entryway and showed the rookies the two taser guns he fired. "Not lethal, guys, but it hurts like hell, huh?" Kenny and Kyle walked to their upstairs command post laughing.

"Kyle, did you put a pacifier in that kid's mouth?" asked Kenny.

"Well he was screaming like a baby when I knocked his legs out from under him," said Kyle.

"Where did you even get a baby pacifier?" asked Kenny.

"Tricks of the trade, brother, tricks of the trade," said Kyle with a smile.

Chapter 5

"Colonel, it's good to see you," said Kyle.

"Your recruits are getting better, Colonel," said Kenny.

"Not as good as you two. It's good to see you, boys; how's your dad?" asked the colonel.

"He's good, Colonel; we'll let him know you said hey," said Kenny.

"Boys, that was good work out there. Your dad would be very proud of you. When I see him next, I'll tell him his boys are still at the top of the game." Kenny and Kyle shared a quick glance at each other. The compliment was well received. "I'll also tell him that your shenanigans are the only things keeping you two from being the best."

"Do you have to tell him that, Colonel?" asked Kenny.

"You two have been gifted with a talent, not to mention you had one of the best trainers in the world for your father," said the colonel.

Kenny whispered to Kyle, "With great power comes great responsibility."

Kyle said, "Shut up, Uncle Ben."

"That's what I'm talking about; everything is a joke to you two," said the colonel.

"That was a movie line, Colonel; a joke is…A blonde in a coffee shop is sitting with her brunette girlfriend and a cell phone rings; the blonde looks at the brunette and says, 'It can't be mine; no one knows I'm here,'" said Kyle.

The colonel smiled and shook his head as if he was just giving up. "You two are incorrigible."

Kenny asked the colonel if this was just the typical once-a-month visit with recruits or was there something else. The colonel handed the envelope of ten thousand dollars over to Kenny, which was the price the government had agreed to pay for every training session. "As you know, boys, I still have a lot of friends in the intelligence-gathering business. Some very interesting information has come up that you two should know about," said the colonel. His expression was somehow very serious then. The room was instantly quiet and the brothers' faces showed nothing but anxious curiosity.

"What have you heard, Colonel?" asked Kenny.

"I would speak to your father about this, boys, but it would be way too uncomfortable for me considering my and your dad's past," said the colonel.

Kyle said, "I thought you and Dad were still friends, Colonel."

"And we are, Kyle, and nothing will change that; it's just…"

"What?" yelled Kenny.

"Kenneth, it's all right, your mom and dad are fine. There was an accident at your mom and dad's house. Well, not an accident, but you know what I mean. A fire in the middle of the night that was supposed to look like your average accidental house fire. Since it was your dad's house, we checked into it. There is a new and not very difficult way to get an ordinary power outlet to start a fire and it is untraceable. We only found it because we had the best looking at it. Your average fire marshal would never catch it. It was a professional job and your mom and dad got out of the house before it was completely lost," said the colonel.

"Mom and Dad's house? What happened? When? Where are they now? Are they OK?" asked Kenny, his voice filled with emotion.

"I told you, they're fine. They're in one of your dad's safe houses," said the colonel.

"The intel, Colonel." Kyle wasted no time. "What was the intel?"

The colonel took a deep breath. "A contract was put out on your father from an unknown."

"An unknown," yelled Kyle. "And you wonder why they call it intelligence."

"That's all we have so far, boys. And from what I understand, the information wasn't received so easily," said the colonel. Kyle wanted an explanation. Sensing this, the colonel simply said, "Ask your father, boys." Kenny asked the colonel how old this information was. The colonel had only just received the information that morning and brought his recruits for two reasons. To test them against the best and for back-up in case someone was on to the Rhoberts boys.

"Any ideas on the perpetrator who got Mom and Dad's house?" asked Kenny.

"Not yet, but they think he might be a local to that area. The information received by Intelligence and the timing on your parents' house is too coincidental. There's only an hour gap between the dissemination of the material and the hit on your dad's house," said the colonel.

"You've got a leak? Is that what you're saying?" asked Kyle.

"I want to say there's no way that it's possible, but the circumstances sure point that way," said the colonel.

"What are y'all doing about it so far, Colonel?" snapped Kyle. The colonel could see the concern in the boys' faces and he was willing to give Kyle the chance to vent, but his time in the military did not warrant a lot of forgiving or allow a disrespectful remark very often.

"I have my own men, whom I trust implicitly, working on it, Kyle. You two need to go see your parents. I'll contact your dad when I get something solid," said the colonel.

"Which safe house are they in, Colonel?" asked Kenny.

"They're currently staying in the Shreveport safe house for now," replied the colonel.

"Then that's where we are going. Kenny, let's get our stuff together and jam," said Kyle.

"Way ahead of you, brother," said Kenny.

Chapter 6

His name was Antonio Fuentes. He was a lieutenant in Special Forces and his tag was "blue leader." Two men handed his team's ass to him today. Colonel Smith did not give much of a briefing and no intel whatsoever. He was not making excuses. His team was not ready and the mistakes they made were entirely their own. The layout of the grounds did not include a tunnel facility that he now knew existed. He did a thermal of the location after they lost. (He did not like to lose.) The colonel seemed to have known the two. Seemed something like family if you asked Fuentes. There was something about those two. The one that came up on blue team's six was very efficient. None of blue team even got a look at them when they were marked. The mystery man's anticipation of their tactics was almost too good. The other that hid in the shadows who marked them seemed a bit more careless, but effective nonetheless. These guys could have be retired Special Forces, he thought. If not, they were provided training by someone with equal skills. They knew blue team was coming and the team treated it like an exercise. Fuentes was sure the place was wired for detection in all sectors. He wondered if anyone had conquered this scenario. Or those two mystery soldiers, for that matter. To Fuentes' surprise, he was not that disappointed. Fuentes wanted to be the best in the game. Blue team was not the best tonight. Fuentes' hope was that he would get to work with these guys again. He also hoped they were on the same side.

Chapter 7

Kenny was hauling all the equipment and weapons, and his brother, in their burgundy-colored 2004 Lariat Ford pickup with the camper shell. Kyle wanted to bring the Hummer, but Kenny thought it would be too much of an eye catcher. The point was to be as covert as possible. There were not too many people out there staring down pickup trucks with camper shells. "Hey, butt-breath, wake up. We're almost there," said Kenny.

Kyle started to wake up and come around. "We pick up any babes while I was out?" asked a groggy Kyle.

"Yeah, but because we have the camper shell on, I'm not sure who really wants us, or is just out for the camper. It is hard to know whom to trust when you are driving a babe magnet like this. There was one woman who passed that was admiring the slobber you were providing on the window. I have a Polaroid of it. She was, like, ninety years old and followed us for a while," said Kenny.

"Can I see the Polaroid?" asked Kyle.

"Gave it to her at the truck stop," said Kenny.

A confused and obviously not fully awake Kyle asked, "The truck stop?"

"Yeah, the truck stop, where you made out with her," said an amused Kenny, having fun with it now.

"You are full of she-it, boy," said Kyle.

"Yeah, well then what's that in your lap, bro?" Kyle looked down in his lap and saw what appeared to be a set of false teeth. He jumped at the sight of them and slapped them off his lap with his right hand.

"Damnit, Kenny! Quit screwing around," said Kyle.

"I was about to say the same thing to you, but whoever you want to see or do is your own business; just don't bring them home. I don't think Mom would appreciate it," said Kenny.

"Hey, Kenny," asked Kyle.

"Yeah," replied Kenny.

"Where did you get those false teeth?" asked Kyle.

"Tricks of the trade, brother…Tricks of the trade," said Kenny.

"My ass, you really did stop at a truck stop! Didn't you, Kenny?" asked a perturbed Kyle.

"I cannot divulge all my connections to you, Kyle. Now if you could stay awake on a trip farther than two miles, I will let you in on all kinds of tricks that you know nothing about. Remember the sleep overs on the bases when we were kids. You were always first asleep. Moreover, that fact says a lot about your personality. You trusted back then, and you shouldn't have. I've been watching your back for years and you didn't even know it," said Kenny.

Kyle was awake now and had got agitated at his brother. "When did you watch my back at any sleep overs?" barked Kyle.

"Let's just say I spared you a lot of tummy aches," said Kenny with a grin.

"Well, I went to sleep on purpose at those parties. I knew you had my back," said Kyle.

Kenny looked at Kyle and Kyle turned away. A few minutes passed and…"You had me at hello," said Kenny, trying not to laugh.

Kyle turned and looked at his brother and said, "*Jerry Maguire*…and you are such a fag! I am telling Mom and Dad. Mom always did want another girl. You can talk about shopping and discounts..."

"Shut it and pay attention; we have a tail," said Kenny.

"Is that why you woke me up? Because someone is following us?" mumbled Kyle. A black Chevy van had been tailing the brothers since Tyler, Texas. Kenny noticed it when he took an exit out of habit to check for a tail and the van followed. He must be new to the game, because he followed Kenny back on to the freeway.

"You want answers don't you?" asked Kenny.

"Yeah, but you know the one following is just a stooge. They always are. If it was someone with talent, we might not have noticed," said Kyle.

"At least inconvenience him for me. Shouldn't he pay the price for following us?" asked Kenny.

"All right Ken, some stop sticks?" asked Kyle.

"Stop sticks are good," replied Kenny. Kyle crawled back in to the camper shell and made his way to the back window. In a long cardboard box, there was a flip top to twelve stop sticks. It was a triangular metal bar with three sides of spikes. The bar had a light paper cover to conceal the spikes. Police issue, which most people can buy at a police supply store. Some of the stores do not exactly ask for identification. Kyle grabbed one and unfolded its first leg. (Think of one of those old time rulers that trifold into one.) It was 4:00 A.M. on Interstate 20 between Tyler and Marshall, Texas. Therefore, no one else was watching. Kyle opened the back window on the camper shell just enough to slide the first leg out.

"When the first leg hits the road, I'm letting it all out. On three, two, one, it's out." The triangular stick flopped out of the truck, rolled for about twenty yards, and rested perfectly across both eastbound lanes of traffic. The driver of the van was 100 yards off. Sixty yards off. Twenty yards off. POP! POP! The van was top heavy but the driver was unfortunately able to keep it from flipping. He came to a stop on the shoulder with the sticks stuck in the right rear wheelbase. (All four tires were flat.) It sucked to be him. Kenny stopped the truck and waited for movement. The driver of the van, and anyone else in it, decided not to make an appearance.

"Happy?" asked Kyle.

"You're the one that should be happy; I just saved you another ninety-year-old lap dance," laughed Kenny.

Chapter 8

The rest of the drive was uneventful. The brothers knew most of their parents' safe houses. (The ones they told them about anyway.) The one in Shreveport they knew well. The brothers were born in it. It's an older home built in the 1960s. In, what used to be, a smaller subdivision. Now it was like every other subdivision, phase one of five. Their mother lived in the house while their father was in Vietnam. John Rhoberts spent three tours in Vietnam and the brothers were born while he was on his second tour. "Why do they call them tours? It's not as if a Vietnamese citizen is driving them in a bus giving them boring historical facts. Sorry. I digress," thought Kenny.

The house was not how Kenny remembered it. (Not that he remembered it at all at that age.) The house was off white with light blue accents. It had a fully enclosed one-car garage. (Wow.) It used to be a covered parking area. The pavement was older with cracks in the sidewalk and oil stains in the driveway. A smaller, thinner sidewalk leading from the garage to the front door was cracked and faded as well. Kenny was going to miss their old house. He parked two houses down from the safe house. Standard Operating Procedure (SOP) for visiting their parents. If they parked in the driveway or right out in front, their father would have given them a speech about safety. Also, the brothers could not possibly know if things were calm in the Rhoberts residence. Growing up in a Special Forces home was a lot different from others. "Wonder if the milkman's kids had to run around with a six pack of bottles in a wire carrying case and not break a single one?" thought Kyle to himself.

"Still dreaming about the lap dance from Wrinkled Rita?" asked Kenny.

"You are a very sick man. Are you ready?" asked Kyle.

"To visit Mom and Dad? Uh, yeah? Wait, we are not sneaking in are we? Because I think that current events may have Mom and Dad on some kind of alert," said Kenny.

"Kenny, you know the place has video surveillance up the wazoo. I would be surprised if Dad doesn't already know we are here. And that's what scares me," said Kyle, sweating a little now.

"You know they're expecting us, so come on. I'm tired and could do with a sandwich or something," replied Kenny, not concerned in the least. However, Kyle saw what he was looking for. They usually did not catch the simple things. The welcome mat on the front porch was elevated. (Booby trap?) Let Kenny go in first. Kenny reached the front doorway and was standing on the mat. Kenny raised his right hand to knock on the door and…their mother opened the door.

"What took you two so long? Your father is about to have a conniption fit because you two are just fiddle fartin' around on the front lawn. Don't you two know about the old house?" asked Barbara Rhoberts.

"Hi! Mom! Yeah we know. It's just that Kyle was thinking that Dad had one of his contraptions waiting for us," said Kenny frowning at Kyle.

"Kyle, get your butt over here and give your mother a hug." Barbara Rhoberts was a caring mother with a strong sense of family and an uncanny way of knowing if you were lying to her. She had a very sweet disposition but it had its limits.

"Mom…What happened to always keeping your guard up? I was checking the perimeter for you two," said Kyle with his head down, trying not to make eye contact with his mother.

"We'll check your reflexes some other time, Kyle; let's just get inside so we can catch up and visit," said Barbara Rhoberts.

"Yes, ma'am," said Kyle.

Chapter 9

"Colonel Smith, have you been able to grade our drill at the apartment complex, sir?" asked Fuentes.

"You mean your failure at the apartment complex," barked the lieutenant colonel.

"Yes, sir, I guess so, sir," said Fuentes.

"You guess so? Come in to my office, Fuentes," said the colonel.

"Yes, Colonel," replied Fuentes. The colonel had his eyes set on Sergeant Fuentes' eyes, neither of them giving to the other. The colonel finally broke eye contact with Fuentes, or he would have run into the hallway wall. Fuentes went in to the colonel's office and faced his desk ready for a battle royale. The colonel slammed the door to his office, sat at his desk and poured himself a small glass of dark rum. He took a sip of the rum, grimaced a little and sat back in his chair just watching Fuentes.

"Sergeant," said the colonel.

"Yes, Colonel," replied Fuentes.

"At ease," said the colonel.

Sergeant Fuentes went to ease but was still stiff as a board. "Sergeant, your squad failed. You failed. However, so has every other squad that conducted that scenario. I did not expect you to win. I am aware of the excuses you want to make and the questions you want to ask. I will not answer your questions. We both know I'm above that." Fuentes thought the colonel a bit too big headed. "However, I will tell you this. Your team got farther than most. You wondered why there was so little intelligence on the mission. Well we do not always get good intel. That was the point. We both know that in most cases you may have been given more intel on what you were facing, how many you were facing and what there capabilities might have been. I did not care for your squad laughing over the radio. That kind of behavior in the field causes others to relax and as your commanding officer, I do not want any squad relaxed in the field. Is that clear, Sergeant?"

"Yes, Colonel," said Fuentes.

"Good, now forget about the drill at the apartments. Your colonel has a job for your squad. If you fail me on this, Sergeant, I'll have you in charge of lawn care at Fort Bragg, get it?" asked the colonel.

"Yes, Colonel," replied Fuentes. The thought of lawn care at Bragg was definitely not good.

"You and your squad will be briefed at 0600 in the main briefing room at HQ. See you then. Dismissed," said the colonel and he waved Fuentes out of his office.

"Colonel," said Fuentes. And with a quick salute, Sergeant Fuentes was out the door. Fuentes was not one to show emotions. Especially after leaving the colonel's office, but he could not help a small grin. He did not like the fact that the colonel would not share information on the identity of the two black ops personnel. It seemed to him that the training those two had received rivaled their own. Still, his squad did better than most, he thought, and the colonel was giving him an assignment. Things were looking up.

Chapter 10

"Boys, welcome home," said retired Colonel Rhoberts (or Dad). Kenny and Kyle embraced their father one by one. The hugs were short because none of the men in their family embraced for very long. (A show of weakness according to their father.) Their mother expected a long hug, but even then, their father would cough or fake sneeze to get their attention. Kenny hung on too long on purpose just so he could hear his father fake some king of bodily noise to separate them.

"Hey, Fath," said Kenny (short for Father).

"Hey, Dad," said Kyle.

"Sit down, boys; let's talk," said Mr. Rhoberts.

"Do y'all want anything to eat? A sandwich or soup or something?" asked their mother.

"Yeah, that sounds great, Mom," replied Kenny.

"You know where everything is then. The refrigerator was well stocked in the Rhoberts home for the visit. I'm going to check on your bedrooms and make sure they are all made up." Kenny winced at the comment. He knew she was going to say that. When Kenny and Kyle were old enough to do for themselves, they were expected to.

Kyle smiled and whispered to Kenny, "You never learn."

"Shut up, Spalding," said Kenny.

"I'm going to tell Dad you just quoted *Madagascar*," said Kyle and he had raised his hand as if to get his father's attention.

"And I'm telling you, grown men and women watch Disney. Most of the jokes in those movies a child would not understand in the first place. They only laugh when a character farts or burps or something, just like you," said Kenny.

"You two finished?" asked Mr. Rhoberts. They both said "yes sir" simultaneously and hung their heads. They knew that their father did not appreciate it when they were clowning around when a serious moment was supposed to be transpiring.

"I've got a pretty good idea about who hit us," whispered their father, evidently trying to keep it from their mother's ears. He had their full attention now. "We don't have a name, but I have a good description and a possible address supplied by a friend of mine. We are sure the address is a ruse, but we will check it out anyway. Here is the best part. This guy is a member of one of those paint ball commando type groups. He's gonna be on the Red tonight for some games" (Red River).

Kenny smiled and looked at Kyle. "A paint ball group!"

"How do we know this is legit, Dad; we don't know who to trust," said Kyle.

"I just told you, Kyle, I trust her," said their father. Kenny and Kyle looked at each other.

"Her?" said Kenny.

"You two still haven't put it together? How do you two get your assignments?" barked their father.

"Dad, you're not supposed to know too much about that," said Kenny, his voice trailing in the end.

"Well I do know all about that. You two have not done anything to shame our family, and from what we understand, there have not been any mistakes. We are very proud of both of you, except for the fact that you have not figured out who your intelligence officer is. Do you two know John Doe?" asked their father with a sly grin on his face.

"How do you know about John Doe? He was initially a contact given to us by Lieutenant Colonel Smith for, um, cleaning up specific problems. Nevertheless, he promised us he would not tell you. It's not exactly what you raised us for," said Kyle with more emotion than he meant to.

"Jane Doe?" asked Kenny. "You've got to be kidding!"

"No. I'm not, and if she were here right now…"

Just then, Kenny blurted it out, "Suzy…Suzy is Jane Doe."

"Our sister is Jane Doe, Dad?" asked Kyle.

"Only family can be trusted," said their father. Kenny looked at Kyle to tell him that their father had just quoted from the movie *Batman and Robin*, but Kyle shook his head no. Apparently, this was supposed to be a serious moment.

Chapter 11

It was 0600 at the headquarters conference room at BOB (Black Ops Base located somewhere in East Texas). Fuentes' squad had been there for half an hour. Colonel Smith entered the conference room about two minutes late. For the colonel, that was about ten minutes late. The colonel seemed upset by the look and color on his face. Whenever he showed those stress lines over his unibrow and his face was redder than it should have been, nothing was going to be good.

"Sergeant Fuentes, dismiss your men; you stay," said the colonel. All throughout the room had seen exchanged looks as blue team members left the conference room without the common courtesy of being asked properly. While the team members filed out, the colonel had rapped his fingers on the table as if the men were not leaving fast enough. This was not going to be good. As the last blue team member left the room, he closed the door behind him.

"Anthony, come sit by me, son," said the colonel in a very soft manner which confused Fuentes. In addition, using Fuentes' first name was a ruse for Fuentes to take the conversation lightly.

"Yes, Colonel," replied a confused but curious Fuentes.

"The assignment I had for your team is a no go. Apparently, our veterans don't count for much these days," said the colonel.

"Colonel, I don't understand," said Fuentes.

"The assignment I was cooking up is not only one of national security, but of a personal nature as well. It's about the latter that I would like to speak to you now," said the colonel.

"Colonel, whatever the job is, I'm in," said Fuentes.

"I know that about you, Anthony. I just want you to know what you're getting into."

"This about those two hot shots, isn't it, Colonel?" asked Fuentes with a concerned look on his face.

"Don't worry, Sergeant, you are not going head to head with those two. On the contrary, I want you to shadow them and protect those two as if they were your own team members."

"You want me to protect them, Colonel?" asked Fuentes.

Laughing a little, the colonel said, "Yes, but it's not only them. They have recently become the target of a very bad group of people known as 'Armageddon.' The resources of this group were vast and their training was similar to that of our own Special Forces. I regret that I cannot share the information as to why the Rhobertses are being targeted, save this: it's about their father and my friend, retired Colonel John Rhoberts. If the need arises, you are to protect him as well."

"Colonel, my team is up to the task I assure you," said a very confident Fuentes.

"Therein lies another problem," said the colonel. "This assignment is not sanctioned by the United States government. Furthermore, You, Sergeant, could not get approval for your team. I'm sending you alone." Sergeant Antonio Fuentes felt the ball drop. He had felt a cold shiver run down his spine as if a ghost had just entered the room. "This assignment is voluntary, Anthony, so take your time and think about it. When you're ready…"

"I'm ready," interrupted Fuentes.

"Very well. As your colonel, I felt the need to make you a simple packet with pictures of the Rhobertses for you as well as known addresses and vehicles they drive. You can find them in the Shreveport safe house, number three on the list, right now. Although, if you hurry, you might assist them in an operation they are working on tonight. I thinks it's right up your alley. I have put it all in your briefing. When you leave here, report to the quartermaster for your equipment. I have filled out the red tape so you can get what you need. Remember that if anyone in our chain asks, tell them you are on a training op. If anyone asks that is not in our chain, tell them to kiss your ass. You have my secure line and you can use it whenever you need to. If you need assistance, call me because I am the only back-up you get. Godspeed, Sergeant, and watch your six," said the colonel.

"Thank you, Colonel. I'll make you proud, sir," said Fuentes, who reached out his right hand for the colonel's hand.

The colonel took his hand, "You already have, Anthony, you already have."

Chapter 12

It was about 2:00 P.M., and Kyle and Kenny were in John Rhoberts' seventies good time van with tinted windows, rear A/C and a genuine 8-track player. Their father had opted to stay at home, in case the arsonist had a file and photo of him. It would not do any good to ID the rest of the family before they had some fun. The house of the flamethrower was in a subdivision called Sunshine Meadows. It was only about five miles east of their parents' safe house. An older brick home with yellow paint on the wood and sided areas. A chain link fence surrounded the back yard and both sides of the home. The fence revealed two pit bulls wandering the property. The fact that the dogs were wandering proved the dogs have not been properly trained. Some of the best-trained dogs will sit at a point where they can watch a majority of the property and watch their master too. With two dogs, you could have three sides of the property watched and the inside of the home if the back has enough windows and open access. These dogs were probably from the pound, or worse, he fought them. Kenny took a closer look with a pair of binoculars.

"Fresh visible scars on the dogs' faces. I really do hate people who fight animals," whispered Kenny.

"I know you do, Kenny, so do I. Let's not forget why we're here, huh?" responded Kyle.

"Well, have you seen any movement, Einstein?" asked Kenny with sarcasm.

"Look, don't get ticked at me because the Human Torch gets off fighting dogs! I don't fight dogs! I like dogs. I hang out with you, don't I?" asked Kyle who tried to lighten the mood.

"Yeah, I guess you're right. Sorry about that." Kenny was not good at apologies. Kyle was not very good at receiving them.

"Uh, you had me at hello! So shut up," said Kyle.

Kenny thought about the movie *Jerry Maguire* while watching the house. A body heat signature was running in the house. It was hard to lock in on anything, because it was ninety-seven degrees outside and the humidity was that of being in a swimming pool.

"May as well use sunglasses. It is too hot to lock in on anything. The roof and sidewalks are lighting up the screen too much," said Kyle.

Kenny looked away from the house at Kyle and blurted out, "Do you think it odd that when Tom Cruise and Cuba Gooding, Jr. are doing that scene in the bathroom, and they seem to be communicating well, but neither one of them really has a problem with Cuba being naked? Moreover, how many takes did it take? Was he naked on every take? Was there a tour of the set that day while they were shooting that scene?"

"Kenny, you have some serious issues," said Kyle. Kyle was going to do the mail carrier gig. His truck was just down the road and Kyle was betting he could beat him to the punch. Just a quick look around. Kyle would be right back. "How do I look?" asked Kyle.

"Like someone about to go postal. No serious, I've always wanted to ask a mailman this, 'When it says fragile on the box, do you guys just chuck the hell out of it 'cause the insurance will take care of it and it "breaks up" what would have normally been a dull day?'" Kenny said with a huge grin.

"We're gonna talk about being serious sometimes on these operations when I get back. In the meantime, wait for me here, don't leave and do not play with yourself on my highway. You can think about it, but don't do it," Kyle said as exiting the van.

Kenny thought for a moment while watching his brother approach the Torch home. "*Smokey and the Bandit,*" thought Kenny.

Kyle approached the home and was shuffling through some old mail that he had found in the trash down the street. He knocked on the door several times but no one answered. Kyle tried the front door knob and it was unlocked. He went quickly inside and closed the door. Immediately after softly closing the front door, the dogs in the back started barking. From the front entryway, however, there was no line of sight to Kyle. "It must be a dog thing about the mailman," whispered Kyle to himself. The inside of the home looked like a large garage sale that had blown over in a storm. The place had a very bad smell to it. Like the water was turned off, then on, and then off again. He had electricity because Kyle could hear the refrigerator humming. "Bingo," whispered Kyle. A guest room with pictures and frames and, uh oh, empty needles, spoons, and candles. They had a drug addict, or a local petty dealer. This was getting better and better. Wait until Kenny heard about this. He would want to stay and wait for the guy. Now they knew about the dogs. Local dealers would keep dogs in the fenced-in property line to keep out the competition and slow down the police. Kyle heard a door open in the back and the dogs were scratching at what was probably a sliding-glass door. "Was this guy sleeping in his garage?" thought Kyle. "Back out the front. Ease the door shut." The front door opened and Kyle was putting the trash mail into the Torch's mailbox. The Torch stood five foot ten, about 160 pounds; long, straight, black, oily hair with eyes that were almost black. He was wearing black boxers and nothing else. He had decently cut features in the abs area. Most of the hard users do, because they do not eat much. "Dude, were you in my house?" said the Torch.

"Nope, just delivering the mail," said Kyle and he remembered how to mess with these guys' minds. "You are in your house."

"I'm in my house?" asked the Torch.

"Yep, you are in your house," said Kyle.

"I know I'm in my house, Mr. Mailman, just give me my freaking mail," said the Torch and he looked at the mail as if he could read. "It's not even my mail, dude. Man, you guys suck," he yelled and he threw the mail at Kyle's feet and slammed the door in his face. Kyle continued to walk down the street putting a piece of trash mail in each box until he reached the corner about six houses down. Kenny was waiting for him in the van at the corner. Kyle opened the door and Kenny was still laughing. Kyle threw his mail hat down and told Kenny that the Torch appeared to be a local drug pusher and addict. Kenny finally stopped laughing and told Kyle he did a good job.

As he turned the van around and headed for home, Kenny said, "But, Mr. Hand, if I'm here, and you're here, doesn't it make it our time, dude?" Kyle looked at Kenny when he said it, then just looked at the road and sighed.

Chapter 13

Sergeant Fuentes was on the road. He was heading east on I-20. "Not a whole lot to look at out here unless you like pine trees, and I do kind of like pine trees," he thought. He picked up a white covert van with a water department sticker on the side. All the equipment he needed was already packed neatly in the van and pre-labeled. He was sure the colonel made the list of equipment and probably had his own blue team members fill the truck. It would have been the quietest way he could think of doing it himself. "How am I supposed to watch these guys when they're well trained to spot a shadow," thought Fuentes. "Only the Shadow knows," said Fuentes to himself. He read that the Rhoberts twins were movie buffs. He liked that about them. He loved movies himself. Maybe this wouldn't be a bad assignment after all. He thought about the training fiasco and remembered thinking that he did want to play on their side.

The intelligence information printed in the office. It was displayed on the third of five computers in the office. Suzy Rhoberts had informants all over the United States and some abroad. Some were provided by Colonel Smith, some by her father and the rest she acquired on her own. This one was local. The printout had information on what turned out to be a local heroin pusher. He had a few arrests for possession and delivery of controlled substances and arson. "Bingo," said Suzy to herself. His dossier was not impressive. She had already found out that this pusher liked to play commando paint ball scenarios with the local wannabes. However, the arson offense was icing on the cake. The informant knew almost too much about the arsonist. "I wonder if this isn't either the competition or a disgruntled user selling the information to my informant," she thought.

She sent the wired payment to the local informant through different channels that included several small businesses in the area. She supported local businesses in exchange for running their bank accounts at no charge to the owners. The owners loved it because they did not have to deal with paying the bills and balancing statements and so on. The bargain was clear to each business owner, however, that if he/she were to tell anyone about the agreement and cause suspicion, the money would be taken and the business closed for good. That seemed to keep most of the business owners in line, except for some of the anal owners, who simply wanted to know too much. For those inquisitory minds, a quick visit from some of the friends of the family, ex-Special Forces to be exact, proved to be more than enough to quell their curiosity. Oddly enough, the paint ball group the arsonist affiliated himself with was none other than "War Games." It seemed that War Games were having a little game tonight on the outskirts of the Red River. The arsonist had already paid his dues to enter the game. Suzy would have to amend their records so that it showed three new members and pay their entry fees for tonight. Suzy hoped Sergeant Antonio Fuentes could be there to join the fray. After having his team's butt handed to them by Kenny and Kyle, Suzy imagined he would like to see them in action from outside the box.

The tracker Suzy placed on his van showed him to be somewhere just east of Marshall, Texas. The colonel set up the tracker for his own interests. He liked to be one step ahead of the troops. In addition, Suzy thought he had a father complex about the men he trained. Kind of sweet of him if you asked her. Suzy promised Colonel Smith not to tell Kenny and Kyle about Sergeant Fuentes, but maybe there was a way she could tell them, without actually telling them. She thought, since their father let the cat out of the bag about her being John Doe and all, she had been waiting to have some fun with her brothers anyway. So far, it had been serious assignments and complete anonymity. Not anymore, baby! She decided to just make up some fun names to ease the tension between the three and the War Games group, paid their entry fees and let the games begin. Oh, how Suzy wished she were there at roll call (provided these wannabe warriors had a roll call). Suzy would bet they did. Anything to make it seem like the real thing. Suzy would bet they did weapons checks and had an on-site EMT in case someone got a hangnail or something. Well, the War Games group would normally have had the advantage, because they had played their games at this location many times. Suzy had already scouted the area and made detailed maps with aerial photography to even the odds. Well, Suzy guessed the odds were not really even. Suzy's brothers were going to have a field day with these people. Let us hope Fuentes stayed clear of it.

Chapter 14

Kenny and Kyle were back at the safe house with their parents. After a light meal of baked white fish and broccoli, that their mother made this time, they were back on the couch with their father.

"All right, boys, this is the scenario. Your sister gave us positive ID on the arsonist. His name is Todd Sears and has not been in the Shreveport/Bossier area for very long. From the look of his criminal records, I would say about five years. The problem is there doesn't seem to be any history of this guy before he came here. And that makes me nervous," said John Rhoberts.

Kenny smiled and said, "You mean like nervous because you have to go to the bathroom and you don't think you can make it nervous, or like the hairs on the back of your neck are standing up nervous?"

"Kyle, hit your brother," said their father. Kyle punched Kenny in the left arm and caused a lump in the muscle to form.

Kenny made no noise and lowered his head, "Sorry, Dad!"

"This isn't exactly a one hundred percent ID, boys, so don't get overzealous until you get some information from him. If he turns and he is the one, well, you know what to do. After you get the information, Kyle," their father emphasizing the last. "And by the way, who told you to make an inspection of the perp's house? You know that if you attend the game tonight, you can't be recognized by Sears or the game is up."

"But because I did enter, Dad, we can confirm that the guy is a low life dealer. Furthermore, in one of his bedrooms where the drug paraphernalia was all over the floor, this guy had photos of homes on his wall. They looked like before and after photos of homes that he had burned. I didn't get a chance to peruse all of them, but even in the off chance he isn't the right guy, we would be doing society a favor," said Kyle.

"He's into dog fighting too, Dad. There were fresh wounds on his dogs' faces as if they had recently been in a match," added Kenny.

"Well then do what you have to do with him when the assignment is complete. After the interrogation, and hopefully there is one, we can't very well leave him alive anyway, can we?" asked their father.

"No sir," said Kenny and Kyle in unison.

"How about an idea of Sear's skills. Do we have any idea how good he is? Whether he has been trained or not? Anything in the last five years that may hint to any training?" asked Kyle.

"Only a resisting arrest report where it was noted in the narrative that it took six police officers to take him down. But in the officer's defense, the guy was doped up on heroin," said their father.

"But this guy was a beanpole, Dad; he looked like a strong wind would blow him over," said Kyle.

"Why don't you fart in his direction and find out, Kyle," said their father.

"Dad, did you just make a joke?" asked Kenny.

"Contrary to belief, I do have a hell of a sense of humor. I had to have one raising you two," said their father.

"So did I," said their mother as she walked back in to the room.

"So, can we be serious for a moment, Dad?" asked Kenny.

"Of course, son, what is it?" And Kenny had everyone's attention, which he loved.

"Do you think Todd Sears shops at Sears?" and Kenny got up to run because their father got up to beat the snot out of him.

Chapter 15

It's ten o'clock at night and clear skies under the Jimmy Davis Bridge. The Jimmy Davis Bridge was one of several ways across the Red River and separated Shreveport from Bossier. This was where they were supposed to meet the War Games group for briefing before the games. A few people had already gathered but according to the locals, they would not actually do roll call until ten thirty. It was still about eighty degrees and the humidity was so high the air felt thick and sticky. The War Games members kept shuffling in minute by minute until there were seventeen present. Everyone was wearing dark green camouflage and had painted their faces. The Rhobertses and one other person were the exceptions, who were wearing lightweight breathable masks. Todd Sears was easy to spot in the camouflage gear. He was as tall and lanky in his gear as he was in his boxer shorts.

"Spotted Sears yet?" asked Kenny.

"A blind man could have spotted Sears in this group, and what's that smell? Do any of these guys know what soap is?" asked Kyle.

"I doubt it. Not to be gross, but there is a rather robust gentleman over there with boob sweat on his shirt already. I'll take him, you take the rest," said Kenny.

Kyle laughed and told Kenny, "I think we'll stick to the plan. You play the games with these people and try to flush Sears over to me on the far east border of their playing field. Keep the rest off of me and out of the immediate area while I ask questions."

"Fine by me," said Kenny. The robust gentleman went to the center of the men and asked for everyone's attention.

"Let's do roll call and welcome a few new members," said Robust.

"What's my name again?" asked Kenny to Kyle.

"Dad said we would know. Not like Dad to leave us hanging like this, but still, he seemed happy about it," said Kyle. Roll call had begun and the names of the group members were like handles given to military pilots. There was Maverick, John Wayne, Cobra, Killer and Justice just to name a pathetic few.

"Serpico!" said Robust. The one other man in the group who was wearing a mask approached Robust and shook his hand.

Sergeant Fuentes made the trip in plenty of time. He was already changed and into his gear by nine in the evening. He was staying in the van, which was equipped with a bed, and rear air conditioning. A solar generator that purred like a kitten powered it. He made it to the designated command post area under the Jimmy Davis Bridge with plenty of time to spare. He noticed the Rhobertses right off when he arrived. They stuck out like a sore thumb with these locals. The only two at the command post with their gear on correctly. He thought they noticed him too from the frequent looks. Maybe it was just because he was the only other one in the group wearing a mask like the Rhobertses. Sergeant Fuentes received a scrambled call from Colonel Smith a little earlier telling him of the War Games group, their rendezvous tonight and the name he was answering to at roll call. He liked the name Serpico. That was a good flick.

It was uneventful until they called some weird names that the Rhobertses answered up to at roll call. Fuentes did not know who gave them the names, but the serious-looking brother didn't seem to like it very much. Fuentes noticed the other tall, skinny one that he was supposed to watch out for. Apparently, he went by the handle Knife. The serious brother followed him in to the east riverbed area. "Better go watch out for him first. The other Rhoberts brother seems to be having a good time. He was the lighthearted funny type. He also knows his movies."

"That Serpico guy moves well. Not sloppy and tired like the rest of these guys. I might have fun with him. Still, there's something about him," said Kenny.

"I know. Serpico was an undercover cop in the movies. Something familiar about that kid," said Kyle.

"Um, I'm not sure I'm saying this right," said Robust. "Bunny and Teddy," laughed Robust and the rest of the men laughed with him.

"That's us," said Kenny aloud. They approached Robust and Kenny shook his hand. "I'm Bunny and this is Teddy, as in Bear," said Kenny to a still-laughing group. Kenny let go of Robust's hand and Kyle shook it with meaning. Robust stopped laughing and looked at Kyle. Kenny noticed the tension and bumped Kyle. Kyle let go of Robust's hand but did not break eye contact. Robust must have seen something in Kyle's eyes because he looked away rather quickly, cleared his throat and welcomed them to the group. He went over the ground rules, which was a first for the Rhobertses. Kenny noticed Serpico paying attention to the rules as well. Maybe this was his first time at paint ball commando too.

"A single chest shot is a kill. All extremities take two shots. Everyone please remember that we do not shoot at the head. The EMT station is here at the command post and is off limits. The game is over when the last man comes in and all of our competitors are accounted for. Good luck to everyone. You have fifteen minutes to find a hole. Starting now," said Robust as he threw down the roll call sheet and began running towards the river. Kenny thought it was hilarious. It was like watching someone turning a paint mixer on with a huge water balloon on it. The Rhobertses watched everyone flee the area in all different directions. All of them, except Serpico. He was still waiting in place.

"He's a cool character," said Kenny.

"Is that fear I smell, little brother?" asked Kyle.

"In your dreams, Teddy. Sears went east southeast of Robust," said Kenny.

"I saw him, Bunny, and I'm on it. Oh, remind me to kick Suzy's butt when this is all over. And Dad should have known better too. Bringing unwanted attention to us," whispered Kyle in a very perturbed tone. Kyle took off in a slow-paced run watching his foot placement.

Kenny looked at Serpico and said, "Hey, I loved your movie. I'd love to stay and chit chat, but I have to go." Kenny paused and waited for a response that did not come. "Yes, well, it's been a distinct pleasure meeting you and I look forward to your next syllable with great eagerness," said Kenny who smiled through his mask as he left heading east.

When he was out of sight, Serpico said with a smile, "That's from the movie *Arthur*." And he followed Kyle's tracks towards the riverbed.

Chapter 16

The fifteen minutes had passed and the games had begun. Kyle heard shots in the distance but paid it no mind. He had already passed Robust about two minutes into the game. Kyle had seen Sears looking for a spot to hide. Sears was continuously checking the trees.

"You trap yourself in a tree, genius," thought Kyle. Sears found a tree marked with a black ribbon tied to it. It was difficult to see in the dark, but Kyle had seen it nonetheless. Sears took the ribbon off the lower branch, stowed it in his gear, and had begun to search the ground at the tree's roots. "I don't believe this. This guy is no paint ball commando. This is where he picks up his heroin. This must be his drop-off point. It makes good sense actually," thought Kyle. "Whenever they play these games, he tells his drop to place the dope in the playing area and mark the tree. He must have given the drop an approximate area or he would be out here all night. Well, too bad for him."

While he was concentrating on the pick-up, Kyle was closing the gap between them. Sears took a quick look around and as he did, Kyle lowered his head and went still. When Kyle goes still, he doesn't breathe and he doesn't move. Sears didn't see Kyle and appeared to be concentrated solely on the package. Kyle had taken out the beanbag gun he had been hiding in his vest. He made a quick look around, closed his eyes for just a few seconds to concentrate on any sounds, and raised the weapon. "You burn down homes, deal drugs and fight dogs. I hope God is watching, because I have a feeling he is going to like this. Anytime I meet one of you punks that's been given the gift of life, by God, and you spit in his face by being the worst kind of human being possible, well, I feel it's my duty to make things right. Oh, man. I am ranting again. I'm certainly no angel. Nevertheless, I respect God for who he is. Oops! Head in the game, Kyle," thought Kyle.

Kyle sighted in Sears' head and as soon as he locked it in his sights, he fired. A hard puff of air sounded as the small beanbag shot from the gun and nailed Sears right in the back of the head. Kyle could see the small bag had hit and moved Sears' hair as it did. Sears went down hard and was knocked out from the impact. You could tell that by the way his limbs went limp. Kyle knelt over Sears and checked his pulse. "Still alive. Good." Kyle whispered in Sear's ear, "Now we play, Mr. Drug Dealer."

Kenny went after Robust for the fun of it. He kept trinkets in his tactical vest just like Kyle with the pacifier. He found Robust hiding in a manmade foxhole with a leaf-covered top. "I made one of those when I was in grade school," thought Kenny. He dropped low and took out a pack of marbles. As he crept forward on Robust, he threw a marble in the opposite direction to attract attention. When he was within five feet of Robust, he heard the hard air burst of the beanbag gun about sixty yards east of his location. "Looks like Kyle is shopping at Sears," thought Kenny. The noise made by the beanbag gun was evidently something new to Robust, so he lifted the top of his foxhole to get a better look at the area in which the sound had come from and paint spattered his chest in three colors. Shot three times in a second.

Kenny was smiling as he ran off to cover his brother when he overheard Robust cursing whoever had shot him. He wasn't smiling because he shot Robust, that was a given. He was smiling because he pinned a coupon for a free double quarter pounder with cheese on Robust's rooftop before he left. Kenny made his way past three others tagging them in the chest as he ran. None of the other players seemed to think it was funny. Kenny thought if he could get as many of the players behind him and not between himself and his brother, then the mission would be accomplished. Kenny stopped to listen for a minute. It was good to get your bearings and listen to the woods for a bit. Kenny could feel something was not right. A yellow burst of paint hit the tree beside Kenny. "No way," Kenny thought, and he hit the dirt, rolled over a dead tree for cover and began a search. He heard another little popping noise and noticed that Cobra was sporting a big red paint ball on his chest in the trees about twenty feet from Kenny.

Cobra was looking at Kenny and said, "You got me, I'm out." Kenny had seen someone move in an opening towards the riverbank. It was Serpico.

"Serpico, why did you that?" thought Kenny. He guessed the angle of the shot from the splatter pattern, rolled to the other side of the dead tree, and had an advantage on Cobra. Kenny hesitated for only a second, and moved on to meet Kyle.

"Serpico had me, but took the harder shot. From his line of sight, it must have been a difficult shot to hit Cobra in the tree. Why not take me? There is definitely something fishy about Serpico. I had better go check on Kyle. If everything is copasetic with Kyle and his buddy, I'm huntin' some po-po," thought Kenny.

Chapter 17

Kenny found Kyle in an area just south of where he heard the gunshot. Todd Sears did not seem to be conscious now, but that was about to change. Kyle had already bound Sears with cling wrap around the arms and legs. You have to twist the cling wrap and make repeated cycles around the head when covering the face. You do not want to suffocate the prisoner...yet. Cling wrap left no fibers for forensics, only a bruise if the prisoner fought the bindings. Kyle reached in to his tactical vest and pulled out an ammonia snap. He placed the snap under Sears' nose and had broken it open. Sears had begun to come around but slowly. There was quite a knot on the back of his head.

"Is everyone out of the game?" asked Kyle.

"Most of them. Serpico is still out there, and get this, he tagged Cobra when we were engaged and took off," said Kenny.

"Well, watch my back while I ask a few questions. When we're done, we'll tag Serpico before leaving if you're still interested," whispered Kyle.

"Hurry up then, Teddy, we haven't got all night," snapped Kenny. Kenny looked down at Sears and noticed that Sears was missing both thumbs. They were field dressed, but clearly just taken off. "Is that really necessary? I mean, this man's hitchhiking days are over now. If he's one of those peace-lovin', weed-smokin', long-haired and drive me around the world types...wait, isn't that what happened to those people in *The Texas Chainsaw Massacre?*" said Kenny to Kyle.

"You never were any good at this," replied Kyle. Sears was looking at both brothers now and from the look on his face, he knew he was in trouble, yet he was confused by their lackadaisical conversation. Kyle opened a white handkerchief and showed Sears his own thumbs. Kyle told him, "Do I have your attention? Nod yes or no." Sears looked at his thumbs and it finally hit him about the pain in his hands. Sears nodded yes and began to cry. "Keep it real quiet, Sears. After all, we have so many more fingers and toes. Simple questions. You get them right and I promise that you will see home tonight. Do you understand? Nod, kid," demanded Kyle. Sears nodded yes, still crying. Kyle took out his survival knife and made a dramatic show of removing the twisted cling wrap that was binding Sears' mouth and tied around his head. Sears remained quiet except for the sobbing. "Did you torch a home two days ago on Camille Street?" asked Kyle. Sears hesitated for a moment and Kyle put his knife close to Sears' right eye.

Sears quickly said, "Yeah."

"Who hired you to do this?" asked Kyle.

"I really want to tell you, sir, but I can't. I don't know," said Sears as he looked to the ground. Both of the Rhobertses knew he was lying. Without hesitation, Kyle covered Sears' mouth with his left hand and slid his knife under Sears' right kneecap. Sears was writhing in pain and tried to scream but was muffled by Kyle's hand. Kyle slowly removed his knife and let Sears' adrenaline take some of the pain before asking again.

"Last chance, kid. Who hired you?" asked Kyle with his face almost nose to nose with Sears.

"O.K., O.K., I'm...I'm a probation member of 'Armageddon'. They said if I torched that house, I would get my membership status and I could stop pushing heroin for them. They promised me a clean record, new house, car, the works." Sears was shaking all over now and looking around as if being watched. Just then, a shot rang out. Not a paint ball weapon but a rifle shot. Kyle went down. Kenny was not sure if his brother was shot or just hitting the dirt for cover like he did. Another rifle shot and Sears' head blew up like a melon. A small entry wound on the front of Sears' head and a very large hole in the back told them the shot came from behind.

"It has to be the drop-off guy. He must have been watching to confirm Sears made the pick-up," said Kyle wincing in pain. Another shot, but this one coming from a pistol. Kenny raised his head for a quick peek and could not believe it. Serpico was lowering a black semi-auto pistol. From the look of the size, a Smith and Wesson .357 was his weapon of choice. Serpico was facing the rifleman's location. Kenny took off in a quick run, took out his own Sig Sauer semi-auto .357 and had the drop on Serpico. It seemed that Serpico was still looking at the dead rifleman.

"Drop it, Serpico, or I drop you," said Kenny using his verbal judo tone. No sense in being quiet now, after those shots.

Serpico dropped the weapon and said, "You're welcome."

Kenny lowered his weapon and said, "What are you doing here, blue team leader? And yes, I remember you. That is to say, I remember your voice."

"My name is Sergeant Antonio Fuentes, sir. I am watching over you two, per Colonel Smith. I'm sure he won't be pleased that I've blown my cover in less than a day," said Fuentes.

"That's between you and the colonel, kid. Now, no offense, but I don't know you, therefore I don't trust you," said Kenny.

"I just killed a man that had you and your brother in his cross-hairs," snapped Fuentes.

"That's certainly what it appears. However, trust has to be earned and appearances are not everything. Walk over to Kyle so we can check on him and eventually we can all get the hell out of here. I'll get your sidearm," said Kenny motioning to Fuentes.

"Very well, sir," replied Fuentes. Kyle was fine. The rifle shot hit him square in the chest. The tactical vest stopped the penetration but still knocked the wind out of him.

"Kyle, you O.K.?" asked Kenny.

"Yeah, fine. Who's this?" asked Kyle.

"You don't remember? This is blue team leader Sergeant Antonio Fuentes," said Kenny.

"Do you speak, Fuentes?" asked Kyle.

"Yes, sir," replied Fuentes.

"Yeah, that's him, Kenny. Colonel Smith sent you to watch over us?" asked Kyle.

"Yes, sir," replied Fuentes again.

"Thanks for the taking out the rifle. And stop calling me sir. We're not the colonel or any other high-ranking officer," said Kyle.

"I say it out of respect, sir. Not to offend you," said Fuentes.

"Well how about we respect this moment by getting Sears untied and in the river. Then maybe we can get the hell out of here. Oh yeah, I'm Kenny Rhoberts and this is my brother Kyle. Introductions are over. Kyle, I think you dropped these when the sniper dropped you," said Kenny while he tossed a pair of women's panties at his brother. Kyle gave Kenny a "go to hell" look and put the panties on what was left of Sear's head. "Kyle, that's going to make the forensics people go nuts. There gonna go off on some tangent about an ex-lover with a dispute over drug money, or a homosexual lover who caught him cheating or something," said Kenny while he winked an eye to Fuentes. Kyle tore open the package that Sears had dug up earlier.

"Clearly, this guy," and Kyle motioned to Sears, "was never going to be a good standing member of the Armageddon group." Kyle showed the others the package that Sears had dug up earlier and it was full of packing peanuts.

"Armageddon basically means the end of the world. So maybe when you become a member, your world dies," said Fuentes to a confused Kyle and Kenny Rhoberts.

"If membership to Armageddon meant death, there would be no members, Sergeant," said Kyle.

"Unless you died and came back," said Kenny.

"We need the colonel and John Doe to fill us in on everything they know on the group known as Armageddon," said Kyle.

Kenny looked at Fuentes and said, "Gotta be a huge waiting list to be in that group. I need to get my name on that list. I'll bet James Dean is in it. Elvis Presley, Ren and Stimpy, or wait, maybe Sam Kinison and John Candy. Those two were my favorites. Why do we find fat people funny?"

Kyle saw the look on Fuentes' face and said, "Yeah, he's always like this. Takes some getting used to, but try not to let the sense of humor fool you. He's the meanest player in the game." Kenny snarled at Fuentes and made a growling noise. "Fuentes, go check the sniper you dropped and come back ASAP," said Kyle. Kenny and Kyle Rhoberts unwrapped Sears' body and left him for the crows. "We leave the sniper and Sears and no one will get too bent out of shape. The wounds match their locations. Plant Fuentes' gun on Sears, over here. The cops around here don't have time for forensic files and bullet trajectories," said Kyle.

"I got him in the neck, sir. He bled out. There was no identification on him or papers of any kind. Do you want his weapon?" asked Fuentes.

"No. Good job, Sergeant. Let's get out of here," replied Kyle.

"We going to leave them here, sir?" asked Fuentes.

"Buzzards gotta eat, same as a worm," quoted Kenny.

"That's from *The Outlaw Josey Wales*. One of my favorite movies," said Fuentes. Kenny and Kyle just looked at each other and smiled.

Chapter 18

Once the Rhobertses were back in the van, they confirmed Sergeant Fuentes' story through their sister, Suzy. They also told her about the conversation they had with Sears, as limited as it was. Suzy was going to find out what she could, get their father up to date, and meet them soon. They gave Fuentes a new .357 semi-auto, and told him where to park his van. They followed him and helped him cover the van with an old tarp. They had taken out some of Fuentes' essentials, put them in their truck and headed for their parents' safe house.

"Why did you nail Cobra in the tree?" asked Kenny.

"I didn't think you saw him, sir," said Fuentes.

"Call our dad sir, not us. O.K.," said Kenny in a friendly way. "And I saw him after he shot the tree. The paint's spatter will tell you just as much as blood's spatter, if you pay attention. The trick was to train yourself on recognizing it and move accordingly in less than a second."

"How do I do that?" asked Fuentes.

"Practice and experience," said Kyle from the driver's seat.

"Good info, thanks," said Fuentes.

Kenny put his right hand on Fuentes' shoulder and said, "The council has given us permission to train you. You will be a Jedi, young Fuentes."

Fuentes smiled at Kenny and said, "That's from the movie *Star Wars*."

"Which one, young Jedi? There are six," asked Kenny.

"The one with the kid and Darth Maul. Part one, I think," said Fuentes.

"The kid? Still much to learn, young one, you have," said Kenny.

"Hey, nerds, let's get some sleep at Mom and Dad's and find out what Suzy and the colonel have for us in the morning, or afternoon," said Kyle.

"There is no information on the Armageddon group on the computer network. Either these guys are really good, or they have excellent connections," said Suzy. Fuentes watched her from across the dining table. She looked to be in her upper thirties to him. She had fair skin, blonde hair, blue eyes and she was very petite. Long, straight hair that was placed in a ponytail and she had slightly swollen eyes.

"This family must suffer from allergies. The brothers both had swollen eyes in the woods last night," thought Fuentes.

"Colonel, have you found anything?" asked Kenny. The colonel was speaking on an intercom on a secure line that Suzy had connected by the time the brothers and Fuentes had woken up.

"Our data banks are the same as Suzy's. They show nothing of this group Armageddon, but we have known of their existence for some time. One of the Central Intelligence Agency's informants spoke of the group a few months ago. Just after telling of the group's existence, the informant was killed. The agent he told was killed the next day in a training accident, or so they say. However, not before he documented everything the informant told him in a report. I'm sending it to you now," said the colonel. The colonel sent the encrypted report he found over a secure fax line that was received by one of Suzy's computers.

"This report doesn't tell us anything other than that the guy that mentioned the group Armageddon was based out of Dallas, Texas. And according to this agent's notes, the informant spent a lot of time in a Dallas jail," said Kyle.

"Did anyone follow up on this report?" asked Kenny.

"Are you kidding? Unless it has to do with Homeland Security, no one is really interested," said the colonel.

"Sheldon, thanks for the help. I appreciate you sticking your neck out for us," said John Rhoberts.

"My pleasure, John. Tell Fuentes to stay put until I call for him," said Colonel Smith. Fuentes was at the table but John Rhoberts motioned for Fuentes to keep quiet.

"Will do, Sheldon. Thanks again," said John. The colonel hung up and silence prevailed in the room. "What does an almost anonymous group, based out of Dallas, Texas, have to do with me and why did they take it out on my house?" said John.

"We'll find out, Dad," said Kenny.

"I'll make a few inquiries about this informant's family, friends, cellmates and accomplices, if any," said Suzy.

"I'll call a friend at the Dallas Water Department to see if this informant has ever paid a water bill and if so, where," said Kyle.

"I'm gonna go to Ms. Barrett's apartment and check her out," said Kenny.

"Who the hell is Ms. Barrett?" asked John Rhoberts.

Kenny got up to leave and Kyle said, "He's quoting from the movie *Ghostbusters*, Dad." Kenny was running for it with his father hot on his tail.

Chapter 19

"Nothing real interesting about the informant's cellmates, but I did find something interesting," said Suzy. The brothers, their parents and Antonio were listening to Suzy while enjoying a few drinks on the back patio. "This informant of the CIA, Michael James, has a brother named Jesse James." Suzy stared directly at Kenny and Kyle. Their eyes were wide with surprise. "The very same Jesse James that's taking an interest in you two's handy work," said Suzy pointing at her brothers. Kenny stood up and started pacing the back yard.

"The cop, Jesse James? Jesse-Boy?" questioned Kenny.

"Yes," replied Suzy.

"His brother was a CIA informant?" asked Kyle.

"Yes, and these questions are getting redundant," said Suzy.

"So we go back to Dallas and question Jesse-Boy," Kenny said, more waiting for a response than actually making a statement.

"We can't question Jesse the way we did Sears. Someone is definitely going to miss a detective and we don't want that kind of attention," said Kyle.

"When I said we 'question' him, I didn't mean we kill him after. Duh," replied Kenny, as a defense mechanism because his brother's comment offended him.

"Take your Ritalin, Kenny," said Kyle. Kenny approached his brother.

"Watch how you talk to me, Kyle. I'm not in the habit of being talked down to," spat Kenny.

"Hey! Guys! It's no big deal. Let's cool it, huh," said Fuentes as he jumped up and stood between the brothers who were standing nose to nose at the time.

"Not a good idea," said Suzy. And Fuentes had just heard her when both brothers grabbed him by both arms, bent his hands back and made him kneel.

"Don't get between us, Ant," said Kenny.

"This is how we fight, kid. It never comes to blows, and this is how we discuss our disagreements. Are we good?" asked Kyle.

"Oh, yeah. We're good. I'm sorry. Definitely didn't mean to interrupt a good discussion. Especially when you guys were making so much progress," said Fuentes.

"I think that was sarcasm. You didn't just disrespect us with sarcasm, did you, Ant?" asked Kenny.

"You mean you recognized it as such?" Suzy asked her brothers. The brothers turned to look at Suzy who was having fun at their expense. That gave Fuentes the opportunity he needed. The brothers relaxed their grip and Fuentes locked his hands around their wrists. He quickly began to stand up, then went limp and used all his weight to pull them off their feet. The brothers collided with one another and went down in the grass. Their father just covered his eyes and pretended to ask God why he was meant to suffer so. Their mother told them that it served them right for bickering with one another. And Suzy would not stop laughing, which annoyed them the most.

"Suzy, you're the biggest pain in the butt," said Kyle. Kenny just stuck out his tongue at her and when their mother wasn't looking, gave her the finger.

"Can we get back on point here?" asked their father.

"Yes sir. I'm sorry, sir," said Fuentes.

"You don't owe me an apology, son. Those two do," as John Rhoberts was pointing at the brothers. "But I know I won't get one, so we'll just move on," said John Rhoberts.

"I can handle questioning Mr. James. I can do the reporter thing, or if he doesn't like reporters, I can do the 'I'm a little interested so ask me out' kind of thing," said Suzy still smiling.

"He definitely doesn't like reporters. We know that from watching him tear a few apart. I think he's a homosexual, Suzy, so you've got a really good chance with that mustache of yours," said Kenny. Suzy stopped smiling and Kyle started laughing aloud in Suzy's face. John and Barbara Rhoberts went inside. They had their limit. Fuentes watched as they argued and insulted each other for another hour. In the end, they finally gave in to her questioning Jesse James. Fuentes could tell in a roundabout way that the brothers were very protective of their sister. He didn't blame them. He would be protective if she were his sister too.

Chapter 20

The brothers took their sister and Fuentes to Dallas in their truck. The trip to Dallas was uneventful and there were plenty of comfortable sitting spaces in the back under the camper shell. Fuentes told the brothers that they were more than welcome to use the van. The brothers thanked Fuentes, but they definitely did not want to go anywhere without their equipment.

Kenny told Fuentes, "It's like having one of those dreams when you're in school and you're naked. Or you are a police officer in a gunfight with an empty gun. Or you've just got out all the makings of a wonderful sandwich, and there's no miracle whip."

Fuentes responded with, "What about when have to go the bathroom real bad, you're in a hurry, you have just finished and there's no toilet paper." Suzy smiled and looked at her watch. She was wondering when the men would start talking about doo-doo. She didn't think her brothers would ever grow up but that is what she loved about them.

Kyle said, "O.K., pet peeve of mine. How about the toilet paper you have to use in the restrooms of stores? They think they are making out because they got this cheap, thin, looseleaf notebook toilet paper, but it takes twenty wipes to clean you."

Kenny was chuckling and responded with, "Yeah, and the paper never tears the way it's supposed to. It always tears vertically and never along the perforations. Sometimes the jokes on the walls are funny. One time, I saw Suzy's name and number on one of the stalls at a truck stop and got sick to my stomach."

"Does anyone have anything close to a plan, providing of course there is a bathroom with nice toilet paper in it?" asked Suzy who ignored Kenny's comment.

"Yeah, we have a plan," said Kyle. "We post up across from police headquarters at 1400 South Lamar. We wait until Jesse-Boy comes out on his lunch break and follow him to the restaurant. You follow in and wag your tail or something."

"Is that it?" asked Suzy.

"Don't underestimate yourself, Suzy. We have faith in you. You should start by saying something about how much you wanted to be a police officer. Or how much you admire those who do the job," said Kyle.

"You're going to want to steer away from that gonorrhea you had. And you have your teeth in, right?" asked Kenny, smiling at his sister.

"What if we don't get anywhere with this?" asked Suzy, once again ignoring Kenny.

"I've thought about that," said Kenny.

"Seriously, Kenny," said Suzy rolling her eyes.

"I am serious. If you can't get any information from him, I want you to drop this and quickly pick it up," and Kenny was holding one of his handmade marble cameras and gave one to Suzy.

"Why would she want to do that?" asked Kyle.

"Because, one, we don't have all year to play patty-cake with Jesse-Boy. And B, he is going to follow her after he sees this camera if we know him correctly. And three, by Jesse following her, we control where the interview takes place," said Kenny.

"That's not bad, but what if he calls for help to watch Suzy?" asked Fuentes.

"This guy doesn't call for help. He is a lot like us in many ways. He will be determined to find out what Suzy's connection is to the killings. The trick is not to let him get a long look at the camera. Let him think in the back of his mind that it may have actually been a marble," said Kyle.

"Can I see one of these marble cameras?" asked Fuentes.

"Sure," said Kenny. Kenny took an older camera out that was not connected to a battery pack and handed it to Fuentes.

"This is really light. Where did you get these?" asked Fuentes.

"You know better than to ask that question, Sergeant," said Kyle.

"You're right, Kyle. Sorry about that, guys," said Fuentes as he gave the camera back to Kenny. Suzy looked uncomfortable. Probably because Fuentes was embarrassed by the question he had just asked. As always, Kenny had something to say on the matter.

Kenny leaned in close to Fuentes, made sure Suzy could hear him, and said, "To put it in really simple terms, you can hollow out a marble, place a very small battery-powered microchip with a lens and transmitter attached and remold the glass to its prior shape. The trick is to keep the battery area charged until you use it. It only lasts about five to ten minutes. When it's done, it's done. You can't recharge them, you can't pick up the signal sent from them or download what they received," whispered Kenny.

"Kenny, can you ever keep a secret?" asked Kyle.

"He would have figured it out sooner or later. What's the harm?" asked Kenny.

"Nothing, you just don't get it," said Kyle.

Kenny spoke louder now so everyone could hear him. "I originally made them for dropping in front of Victoria Secret models. Problem is, I never ran into any," said Kenny.

"Playboy models would have been nice too," said Kyle.

"Or pretty girls at the local Macy's lingerie section, huh?" asked Fuentes.

"Now you're talking," said Kenny. Suzy was wondering how long it would take to get to police headquarters. It could not be soon enough.

Chapter 21

"Can we at least keep the air-conditioning on? I need some kind of circulation back here. And Kyle, if you ever eat beanie-weenie again, I swear, I'll kill you," said Suzy waving her right hand in front of her nose. Kyle gave Kenny and Fuentes thumbs-up and smiled. Kenny had an oxygen mask on and Fuentes was turning green. The Rhobertses and Fuentes arrived at Dallas police headquarters just before 9:00 A.M. They found a parking lot that was unattended, parked as close to the police entrance as possible and put money in the corresponding receptacle. From then on, Suzy would be in hell. It was quickly approaching lunchtime and Suzy Rhoberts was very thankful. From 10:30 A.M. to 11:00 A.M., Suzy was getting ready for her "blind date." She had made up her mind, after looking in the mirror, that Detective Jesse James was not going to be a problem. Oh, she wasn't arrogant in her mind, just confident. She had something to prove to her brothers. They fought long and hard to explain to her that working a source over the computer was very different from getting information from a trained police officer. What she had to make them understand was not all the sources were obtained over a computer and she had taken her fair share of risks.

"Doesn't matter now," she thought. "I want to keep my head in the game. I can see the prize and I...Good grief! Just a little time with Kenny and Kyle, and I'm bantering just like the two of them."

"There he is," said an excited Kyle.

"Yeah, that's him," said Kenny with less excitement and a disapproving look at Kyle. Suzy was out of the van as soon as Kenny made positive I.D. on Detective James. She was going to keep eyes on, until James either got inside an unmarked car or picked a spot to eat. The Rhobertses noticed early upon arriving at police headquarters that there was a sandwich/burger joint across the street. The hope was that Detective James would decide to eat close to work today. The hope paid off for them.

"At least it's not a donut shop," said Kyle. Kenny was still upset at Kyle for showing excitement at Detective James' arrival. Kenny showed his discomfort with Suzy doing this. Kyle was too, but showing less than Kenny.

"How horribly cliché of you to bring up donuts. Is that how your simplistic mind deals with stress?" snapped Kenny.

"Yeah, I'm worried too, Kenny. But she'll be fine," said Kyle, clearly blowing off his brother's snide comment.

Fuentes, in an effort to create levity, said, "Looks like he's going to eat at the local choke-and-puke."

Kenny said, "Yeah, looks like it. And that was from *Smokey and the Bandit*."

Suzy followed Detective James into the "Burger Bar" restaurant. She let several people get between them in the ordering line. She maintained eye contact with him when he looked, but tried not to overdo it. While standing in line, Suzy realized something that was overlooked in her brothers' strategy: the fact that this particular restaurant was across from police headquarters, that there was ninety-percent men in the Burger Bar, and the subtle eye contact she was trying to maintain with Detective James was near impossible with most of the patrons eyeing her.

Suzy overheard Detective James order a number-one combo. She looked at the menu and noticed that it was a cheeseburger and fries. Suzy ordered the same thing. After getting herself a bottle of water, she found a table to herself and waited. She was number 118. Assuming that the numbering system wasn't different in the Burger Bar than it was at any other restaurant, she was confident of the fact that Detective James' number would be 116. Suzy was surprisingly relaxed at this place. It was intimidating to her to be so outnumbered by men at any place. However, the fact that they were on-duty police officers made it kind of a comfort.

"Number 116," said the teenager behind the counter. Suzy got up and approached the counter.

She arrived just before Detective James and asked the employee, "Is that the cheeseburger combo?"

"Yes, ma'am," said the teen.

"Wait a second. I ordered the cheeseburger combo too. And I think I'm 116," said Detective James a little confused, but holding out his number to the teen nonetheless. Suzy did her best at feigning embarrassment and even attempted to make her cheeks red. (She thought of Kyle's gas.)

"I am very sorry, Officer," looking at James in the eyes. "I lost my number and was watching the counter for a cheeseburger combo. I must be the next one," and Suzy turned to sit down.

"Wait! Why did you call me an officer?" asked Detective James. Suzy had her back to him and smiled.

She turned slowly back around to face him and said, "A man eating across from a police building wearing a shoulder holster in a crowd like this is either suicidal or a policeman." Detective James looked at his holster and just remembered that he took off his coat and placed it on his chair at the table.

"It's a little embarrassing to admit this now, but I'm a detective, not an officer," said James.

"I don't really know the difference," said Suzy, leaving a huge opening for Detective James.

"Could I explain it over lunch?" asked James. Suzy gave him a slightly concerned look and acted as if she was unsure. "I promise I won't arrest you," said James.

"Okay," said Suzy. "You don't look like the suicidal type to me."

"Wait until you eat the cheeseburger, then try and say that again," said James. Suzy gave a convincing laugh and followed Detective James to his table.

Chapter 22

Kenny and Kyle waited for what they thought was an eternity for Suzy to finish lunch. They finally watched her exit the restaurant with Detective James walking out next to her. Suzy was smiling, laughing, and even touched Detective James' right shoulder once. Fuentes thought she was obviously hamming it up for her brothers. Then the hope that was present shattered all at once. The brothers watched as their sister tried to make a clean break. Suzy turned without looking and ran right in to a policewoman that could have been mistaken for a brick wall. Suzy accidentally spilled all of her purse's contents onto the pavement. The policewoman kept walking and Detective James gave the woman a dirty look. Suzy quickly began searching for the marble camera. Detective James bent down to help pick up the contents when his eye caught the marble. He quickly grabbed the marble and examined it. He began to look at Suzy very hard and would not break eye contact. Suzy pretended not to notice the stare and thanked him for his assistance.

"That statement is too cold. You should have thanked me for

eyeing the fat woman that bumped you. Who are you and what are you up to, lady?" asked Detective James as he closed the gap between them.

"I beg your pardon?" asked Suzy with a surprised look as she took a step back.

"It's a given that I'm not the most attractive guy in the restaurant. I have even tried the menu pick-up once myself. But I've never had a discussion with any woman who wanted to know so much about me on what initially appeared to be a first encounter," said Detective James calmer than Suzy expected.

"Look, I don't know what..." attempted Suzy until James cut her off.

"The camera, lady," whispered James in a very subdued yet angry way. He approached Suzy, grabbed her by the upper right arm and had begun to forcibly pull her out of view from the dining officers. "Where did you get this camera?" James yelled at Suzy so absorbedly, he was leaving spit hanging from his mouth. The sound of squealing tires made James turn his head in curiosity. He saw what looked like a red Ford pick-up speeding towards him. Before he knew what happened, Suzy snapped James' arm off hers and gave him a palm strike to the nose. The blow to James' nose did not break it, but caused him to lose sight for a few seconds due to his eyes watering.

"You should never have grabbed me like that, Detective Jesse James," said Suzy in a very calm voice, her brothers pulling up alongside them now. Fuentes had the back gate open and Kenny lifted Detective James off his feet and slammed him in to the back of the truck. Kenny put James' head to the floor while Suzy jumped in and closed the gate.

"Sergeant, hold his head down and secure him," said Kenny. Fuentes did it without answering.

"Unfortunately, friends, this little charade did not go unnoticed," said Kyle looking through the rearview mirror.

"One thing at a time, bro," said Kenny. Kyle watched as the restaurant emptied nearly thirty police officers. Only half of which were wearing uniforms.

"This is going to get sticky really fast," said Kyle watching two marked squad cars drive by them in the opposite direction and both made bootleg turns.

"Well, you studied the map before coming here. Find a way," said Kenny. Kenny reached into a bag, got out his Propofol syringe and found a vein on James' right arm. Kenny eased the needle into a vein on James' arm. "Good night, Jesse," said Kenny. "Touch my sister again and I'll kill you." The back of the truck disappeared in James' eyes and all went black. Suzy and Kyle noticed Fuentes had a look of concern on his face. Kenny turned to his sister, "Was it the marble camera?" he asked Suzy.

"Yeah, this guy is really good. We're in trouble aren't we?" asked Suzy with the same look of concern.

"Not as much trouble as Kenny and I were in when we broke Mom's wine glasses and buried them in her garden," said Kyle. Suzy relaxed when Kyle made the joke. Fuentes wondered how he would explain jail to Colonel Smith.

Chapter 23

"Turn on the police scanner, Kyle. Let's hear what they're saying," said Kenny.

"What was that, Kenny? I was listening to the police scanner," said Kyle.

"Can we all hear it since all our butts are on the line?" asked Fuentes.

"Easy, Sarge. We'll lose these Smokeys," kidded Kyle.

"You guys are quoting while we're in a police chase?" asked Fuentes.

"When life gives you apples…" said Kenny before being cut off by Suzy.

"He just wants assurance that we're not going to jail."

"In that case, I assure you that we," as Kenny motioned to his brother and sister, "are not going to jail." Four Dallas squad cars were running lights and sirens behind the Rhobertses now. "We have to lose them before their helicopter gets a bead on us," said Kenny.

"We will," said a very confident Kyle as he drove in and out of traffic heading north on Interstate 35E. The police scanner revealed what the Rhobertses were hoping not to hear. One of their own was taken in a daring daytime kidnapping. What was worse, was that it happened in front of police headquarters. Kyle made periodic exits off the interstate and took side roads that would get him to the destination he had in mind.

"I'm slowing down a little so get the sticks," said Kyle.

"I already got them out. Say when," said Kenny.

"When," said Kyle. Kenny raised the glass window on the back and let the first leg out. When it made contact with the road, he let the rest of the sticks out, pouring three of them on the road. The first two squad cars hit the stop sticks together and were lost in the smoke from the braking tires. The squad car following the first two hit the rear squad car and the driver lost control. Thankfully, no one looked injured from what the Rhobertses could tell. The Rhobertses liked police officers and did not want a single one of them hurt.

Now that the squad cars that were following them were out of the picture, Kyle traveled north on Harry Hines Boulevard. He took a left turn onto Northwest Highway and a right on Shady Trail. He found the public storage that he and Kenny privately owned and hit the remote they kept in the truck to open the gate. He made their way to the back and Kenny jumped out and raised the door to 210. Kyle drove in to the garage storage unit and parked. Kenny slammed the door shut and hit the lights. There were doors connecting five of the storage units that the brothers kept empty and would not lease.

They all got out of the truck and Kenny gave out instructions. Kyle and Fuentes emptied the equipment from the truck and Suzy cleaned all markings in and out of the truck. Kenny was monitoring Detective James and the time they had remaining with the sedative. There were two other cars owned by the brothers in the conjoining storage units. The plan was to clean and leave the truck. They took off the license plates and took them with them. They wouldn't use it again for quite some time and would more than likely have a paint job on it before using it again, if ever. Kyle didn't like to use the Humvee because he thought it brought too much attention to them but there was little choice. They needed the room for their equipment and for their unwilling guest. The Humvee was black with tan interior. The windows had limousine tint on them and had a defroster as well. The vehicle had a full tank of gas and was periodically serviced by Kyle for just such contingencies.

They moved without pause in case there were witnesses to the chase who might have been reporting their last known location. It took the Rhobertses and Fuentes thirty minutes to clean and empty the truck. The Humvee was loaded and so was Detective James, in more ways than one. After a quick peek on the monitors that watched all angles of the property, they left. There were no followers and Kyle took Interstate 35E south just to see if the hornets nest had died out. It hadn't. There were police helicopters and news helicopters like flies at a picnic. Kyle made his way towards Interstate 20 for the three-hour drive back to Louisiana. There would be a modicum of relief when they crossed the state line. Until then, Kenny would monitor Detective James. Suzy was listening to the police scanners, both local and state. Kyle was concentrating on the road and Fuentes was cleaning the weapons and preparing for an interrogation of Detective James.

Chapter 24

The Rhoberts family owned a four-bedroom home out at Lake Bistineau in North Louisiana. They rarely got a chance to use it, but tonight was a good night. Lake Bistineau was about thirty minutes southeast of Shreveport, Louisiana. The lake home was hidden in the woods on the west side of the lake. The house sat in the middle of twenty acres of property owned by the brothers. Along the perimeter of the property, as you might expect, there was a chain link fence with barbed wire at the top. Sensors were placed all over the fence and at strategic places on the property. Kenny and Kyle had a horrible time adjusting the sensors not to react to small animals and alligators. The property was also covered with surveillance cameras that could be monitored from the living room in the house. Most of the cameras were located in the trees and sent the images back via wireless remote.

The Rhobertses built many upgrades into their home, all of which were to help keep the family safe. The wooden home was burgundy in color with royal blue shutters and accents. It was a two-story house with five windows in the front. All the windows had the solar screens on them. They were definitely not in need of solar panels in the woods; however, they made excellent cover. The grass in the yard was non-existent. It's difficult to get any grass to grow in woods this heavy. Pine needles littered the ground everywhere you looked. The wooden-looking home was just that on the outside. The wood, windows, front and back doors, all of it was just a shell to cover the real shelter. Fuentes was about to be very impressed.

They pulled up to the outside gate that had a magnetic lock, which could only be opened by remote. Kyle hit the remote that was hidden in the center console of the hummer. They made their way back into the property taking a path that wasn't identifiable from any other. They began to approach the burgundy-colored wooden home and Fuentes said, "That's a nice place."

"You have no idea," said Suzy. Kyle pulled the Hummer into an old, rickety-looking one-car garage. It looked like it was converted from a small barn. It had a dirt floor and cobwebs all over the place. There wasn't even a gate to pull aside. The colors matched that of the house but were a bit more faded. Fuentes noticed that Kyle pulled inside the barn very carefully and that he was watching his tire placement. When Kyle came to a stop, Kenny told Fuentes to watch Detective James while he looked around. That is exactly what Kenny did. He walked around the Hummer and was checking the tires. Kenny gave Kyle thumbs-up and Kyle hit another remote. A large humming sound began and the Hummer began to sink underground.

When the Hummer stopped descending, they were thirty feet below the surface. Kyle drove off the dirt-covered elevator and sent it back up to Kenny. Kenny was waiting for its return so that he could cover any lines that might show after using the elevator. The lines were minimal and Kenny brushed the old dirt back over them to help conceal the elevator. When Kenny was finished, he simply went out of the barn and proceeded to the back wall. There was a fifty-gallon propane gas tank with rust spots all over it sitting on a concrete base.

Kenny lifted a dead bush out of the way, pulled a tiny lever that was located underneath it, and the propane tank and concrete base lifted on one side to reveal a small set of stairs that went down.

When Kenny arrived in the underground garage, the others were already unloading the Hummer. Fuentes was still looking around the garage in amazement. Fuentes thought there was enough room in this underground garage to park twelve cars. When Kenny finished powering up the lights, Fuentes could not believe it. There were eight motorcycles and ATV's on the other side of the garage. There two Kawasaki Prairie 700 four-by-fours, two Kawasaki Bayou 400 four-by-fours, two Honda CRF250X motorcycles, one red Kawasaki Ninja ZX-14 and last but not least, his favorite, a custom black and gold Harley Davidson XL 1200C Sportster. The Prairie and Bayou models were ATV's with front and rear racks.

"Fuentes! You and Suzy come over here and get on these Bayous. Kyle and I will take the Prairies. Let's load them up and get to the house," said Kenny. When they got close to the bikes, Kyle made sure that Fuentes knew the Ninja was his. Kenny laughed and said to Fuentes, "He's actually proud to tell you that he owns that fast little rice burner. The Harley Sportster is mine, and no, you can't ride it." They loaded up the ATV's and headed down a short concrete tunnel leading them to an area with six parking slots. There was plenty of room for the ATV's to park and unload.

Fuentes noticed two other tunnel entrances. "Can I ask where those two tunnels go?" asked Fuentes.

"Yeah, I guess so," said Kyle. "The tunnel on your right leads to a shack close to the pier where our boat is. The tunnel on your left leads to just outside the fenced-in area on the south side of the property. The stairs in front of you go up to the house."

Kenny placed his hands on his hips and said, "Kyle, you just can't keep a secret."

Kyle said, "Well he's here now and he'll need to know all entry and exits, won't he?"

"He can do just what he's been doing and follow us wherever we go. It's like having my own shadow," said Kenny with a grin at

Fuentes. Fuentes was still looking at the Kawasaki Bayou he just rode and did not hear Kenny. "You want to be alone with that Bayou, Fuentes?" said Kenny.

Kyle started laughing as Suzy looked at Fuentes and her brothers and said, "Boys and their toys."

Chapter 25

The house was unlike anything Fuentes had ever seen. There were three floors in the house. A basement, where they carried Detective James, and a first and second floor. The basement was vast and much bigger than the house looked from the outside. There were computers and monitors all over the east wall on metal stands. After a closer look, Fuentes noticed that the monitors were showing all points around the property. There were fence line cameras and rooftop cameras and cameras in trees. "Who the hell are these guys?" thought Fuentes.

"Hey, Sarge. Give us a hand with James, huh? I'll give you the tour in a minute," said Kenny. Kyle motioned for Fuentes to take the right arm of Detective James and as he did, Kyle walked off towards a private room. Lights came on in the room and several more computers and monitors flicked on. Some high-toned beeping noises and the entire floor was lit up. Kenny was leading James, with Fuentes' help, to a concrete room with a giant door. A single metal chair sat in the center of the concrete room and it was bolted to the floor. Kenny led Fuentes to the chair and they put Detective James in it. Kenny secured James' hands behind his back with handcuffs and told Fuentes to get his legs. Fuentes noticed leg cuffs attached to the chair and secured Detective James. Once James was secure, Kenny checked his pulse and respiration and seemed to be satisfied.

"We'll hook him up in a minute or two. He'll be out for a while anyway. How about that tour?" asked Kenny.

"Sure thing," said Fuentes. Before leaving the room, Kenny wrapped a Velcro strap around Detective James' head and secured it to the top of the chair.

"We want to limit his movement in case he wakes up before we get back," said Kenny. They left the room and went in to the adjoining room that Kyle was still powering up. There were cameras that matched the ones on the east wall and cameras in the room where they just deposited Detective James. "Is the place secure?" asked Kenny.

"Yeah, we're good," said Kyle. "Ready for the tour, Sarge?"

"I'm already on it, brother," said Kenny.

"Well, I'll go with. I never get tired of showing off this place," said Kyle. Kyle and Kenny showed the rest of the house to Fuentes. The first floor was full of free weights, a sauna, showers and a running track that had rubber footing. The track was built around the outside perimeter of the room.

"This is obviously where we would work out, if we did work out," said Kenny.

"It's pretty awesome," said Fuentes.

"But wait, there's more," said Kenny.

"The walls in here are three feet thick with iron studs and concrete filling. The shell on the outside is just that. A shell. We have no windows and no doors except those which we came through from the basement," said Kyle.

"What he's saying is, she'll take a licking and keep on ticking," said Kenny. They led Fuentes to the second floor through another staircase. The second floor had a kitchen, a living room with a large screen television and four separate bedrooms. Suzy was in the kitchen making herself something to eat.

"You guys hungry?" asked Suzy.

"Don't do it," said Kenny to Fuentes.

"Yeah, I'm hungry," said Fuentes.

"Well, you know where everything is now so make yourself something to eat," said Suzy with a smile. Kenny and Kyle smiled at each other.

"I told you not to do it," said Kenny.

"I should've seen that coming," said Fuentes shaking his head and smiling back at Suzy.

"But did you see this coming," asked Kyle. Fuentes watched as Kyle flipped a switch and looked up at the ceiling. The ceiling looked like an oval piece of glass. Fuentes watched as the roof tiles he had seen from the outside of the house fold into themselves and lowered further until you could see the entire sky.

"It's a nice night. You can't see a sky like this in Dallas," said Kenny. Fuentes could not believe it.

"The glass is triple layered, carbon based, bulletproof and magnifies on any particular point by just moving the joysticks over here," said Kyle as he motioned to a chair that looked like a La-Z-Boy with joysticks on both arms. Kenny ran to the chair so he could be first to show Fuentes how it worked.

"Come over here for a second," said Kenny to Fuentes. "But not too close; the chair has to be raised." Kenny flipped a switch on the bottom of the chair. When he sat in the chair, it raised three feet and angled itself towards the roof. "You noticed when you entered, I hope, that there were no cameras watching the sky," asked Kyle to Fuentes.

"Yeah I noticed that," said Fuentes who had not noticed at all.

"It's all right. A little too much to take at once," said Kyle. Fuentes nodded.

"This chair isn't just for star gazing. It's linked to five handmade .45-caliber machine guns with more rounds than Rambo. Flip the switch on the right joystick and your target cross appears. Whatever you see, you kill. The triggers are self explanatory," said Kenny. "The switch on the left joystick is actually for star gazing. Pick a star and close in on it. Use the joysticks to magnify the specific area you want to view. If you like the view you've found, simply pull the trigger on any of the two joysticks, uh, while it's in star gazing mode, and it'll print on the color printer in the corner," said Kenny pointing to the northwest corner of the room.

"Where did you guys get this stuff?" asked Fuentes and as he said it, he remembered Kyle telling him earlier not to ask those questions. Fuentes looked at Kyle and said, "I don't need to know!"

"You're learning, kid," said Kyle smiling back at him.

"So, can I try it out?" asked Fuentes.

"In a little bit," said Kyle.

"Yeah, plenty of time for the chair," said Kenny. "Let's check on Jesse-Boy in our other chair."

Chapter 26

Detective Jesse James woke up in a concrete room with a drain in the center. His hands were cuffed behind him and his feet were cuffed to the chair. The chair was bolted to the floor and was not very comfortable. There were two electrodes connected to both sides of Detective James' temples and a finger clamp on his right index finger. A blood pressure cuff was connected to his upper left arm and he noticed he was extremely thirsty. There was a large flat screen monitor sitting on a metal stand about ten feet in front of him and a single light in the room above him that flickered annoyingly. "Stop messing with the light switch," growled Kyle to Kenny.

"Just having a little fun. He wouldn't have woken up if I hadn't started playing with the lights anyway," said Kenny. They were in an adjacent room watching Detective James from a small camera located inside the interrogation room. The camera was painted to look like part of the wall. It could be seen, but you would have to be looking closely for it. They sent Fuentes in the room to throw off Detective James.

Before allowing Fuentes to go in, the Rhobertses trained him how to ask the questions they wanted answered and what body language to look for while questioning him. If Detective James initially thought that Suzy was family, then the appearance of Fuentes would throw him off. The Rhobertses gave Fuentes specific instructions to follow. He would not be allowed to answer any questions from Detective James. They did not want to have to explain all their past assignments to Fuentes. One, it was none of his business; B, they didn't have the time or energy to explain; three, sooner or later Fuentes would make a mistake on a detail from one of their previous operations and the jig would be up; and D, they didn't trust anyone completely, except their own family.

Fuentes entered the room through a steel door that squeaked loudly like one from a haunted house. The Rhoberts brothers loved it because it was actually intimidating to some of the people who spent time in the interrogation room. Fuentes stepped up to Detective James and both made eye contact.

"This is very simple," said Fuentes. "I ask a question and you give me a straight answer. If you remain silent or I think you're lying, I'll leave this room and you will be punished. Do you understand?"

"Kiss my ass," spat Detective James.

Fuentes turned around to leave the room and said, "Sarcasm and insults count as wrong answers." The door closed behind Fuentes and a small opening appeared in the wall facing Detective James. Two loud bursts from what sounded like an air gun pelted Detective James in the chest with two mace balls. They were comparable to paint balls in size but contained concentrated mace. The Rhobertses and Fuentes watched as Detective James coughed and spit. After a few minutes, Detective James' nose began to run and snot poured from his nostrils. Ten minutes had passed and two fans on the ceiling turned on in unison and cleared the room of mace. The fans forced the air outside, much like a dryer vent. The door opened and Fuentes returned with a bucket of water. Fuentes put his clipboard down and threw the bucket of water on Detective James' face.

After the coughing and spiting began to slow down, Fuentes repeated himself, "Do you understand now?"

"I've been maced before, asshole. You'll have to do better than that," responded Detective James. Fuentes again turned around taking his empty bucket and clipboard with him and left the room. Another opening in the wall facing Detective James and a gas grenade was tossed in to the room. It began dispensing gas about five seconds after hitting the floor. Detective James began to cough and spit again and his eyes were watering and swelling up. Another ten minutes had passed and the overhead fans came on again to clear the room. Fuentes waited an additional ten minutes before entering the room again with another bucket of water. He approached detective James and threw the bucket of water on his face again.

"This water has two purposes. One, to assist in your recovery; and two, you will notice a fair amount of water on the floor now. You will also notice that your chair is wired," said Fuentes. Detective James looked down to see that the two front legs of the chair were truly wired.

"I suppose you're going to electrocute me now?" asked James.

Fuentes turned around to leave the room again when Detective James said, "Just out of curiosity, what do you want to know?"

Fuentes turned to face Detective James and said, "You should know that I don't enjoy this, but there are rules in this room. No one wants to see you get hurt, but that is exactly what will happen if you do not cooperate. We'll start with something simple. Who is Michael James?"

"He was my brother and he was murdered. I know what the Feds say about the incident but I also know that they are full of shit; what do you care?" said James.

"What did your brother do to get himself murdered?" asked Fuentes ignoring James' question.

"From what I understand," said James, "he was an informant for the CIA. I imagine it was as simple as ratting on the wrong people that got him killed." Fuentes' pager went off while in the room with Detective James, which was a signal for him from the Rhoberts brothers to leave the room. When Fuentes left the room, Kenny told him that Detective James was lying. His blood pressure went up and the lie detector was doing the Mambo. The Rhobertses set the stun gun on low. The leads to the stun gun were the wires attached to James' chair. The pulled the lever on the stun gun and Detective James jumped in his chair and let out a muffled scream. The jolt lasted only five seconds but to Detective James it seemed like an eternity. Fuentes let ten more minutes pass and entered the room once more. Fuentes approached James and took a knee so that they would be eye to eye.

"Want to try that last one again?" asked Fuentes.

"My brother was a bit of a nut. He always wanted his name to be Frank James like the real brother to Jesse James. He did his research and believed many of the James brothers' actions were justified. Some press stories made the James brothers out to be folk heroes. In my opinion, they were murderers. I know of only two examples that my brother brought to my attention. The first was when the James brothers joined Quantrill's Raiders and took part in a massacre of two hundred men and boys in Lawrence, Kansas. The second was in September of 1864 when the James brothers killed twenty-two unarmed Union soldiers that were returning home on leave. According to my brother and some encyclopedias, the Union soldiers were pulled off the train and executed in what became known as the notorious Centralia Massacre," said James.

"And what does this history lesson have to do with your brother?" asked Fuentes. Detective James looked perturbed as he felt he had to explain something that was painfully obvious.

"Have you ever heard the phrase, 'The south will rise again'?" asked James.

"Yes. What about its connection to your brother?" asked Fuentes.

"My brother was part of some fanatical group that wanted to make that happen. They supposedly had allies in top-ranking positions in the government. They were even said to have had unlimited funds from some of the larger corporations," said James. "And don't bother asking me about who the political figures were or the corporations involved. I have no idea and they did not share that information with my brother. My brother was a low-level enforcer and wasn't privy to any of that information."

"You're a cop, aren't you? Why didn't you look into this?" asked Fuentes.

"Yeah, start making inquiries into an organization that only a few know about and my brother is a member of. That would go over well with the chief of police. Not to mention the fact that anyone caught discussing this group openly ended up at the morgue," said James. "After my brother was killed, I wanted to make some inquiries. Nevertheless, the reality was, I'm just one man against an army of fanatics. I wouldn't know where to start."

"Did your brother tell you anything that would help you find this group?" asked Fuentes.

"Let me set the record straight on my brother before we go any further. He may have started out believing in this group, but he called me just before he was killed and he was concerned about some of the group's recent activities. I think my brother wanted out," said James.

"Are you avoiding my question?" asked Fuentes.

"No. I just wanted you to know that my brother was not all about this group in the end. He may have had a racist ideology, but it was obvious to me the group was headed in the wrong direction. The only other additional information my brother gave me was not entirely spoken. Like I said before, he called me just before he was killed. The caller ID on my phone listed a 'private caller' but the number was listed anyway. I was able to criss-cross the phone number on our computers at work and it came back to an address in McKinney, Texas. That's about forty-five minutes north of Dallas. I went by the location and it appeared to be a ranch with about two hundred acres. A security fence surrounded the entire ranch and the entrance had a guardhouse with two guards. That's all I know," said James.

The door opened and the Rhoberts brothers entered the room. Fuentes was shocked that they came in to the room. Fuentes backed up against the wall and let the Rhobertses take over. Detective James noticed this and watched both brothers very closely.

"It's you two, isn't it? You guys are the ones offing the deadbeats in Dallas?" said James.

"Your life hangs in the balance, Detective James. The answer to the next few questions will determine whether you live or die," said Kyle. Detective James became very still. He knew what these two men were capable of and if they wanted him to disappear, he was sure they could do it. Detective James could see the intensity in both men's eyes. They also had remarkable similarities.

"No," thought Detective James as it finally hit him. "Brothers," mumbled the detective to himself but a bit too loud.

"That's right. It appears to us that you want to avenge your brother but don't have the capabilities or know-how. Are you willing to use your connections in the police department for a limited time to assist in avenging the death of your brother provided you had the best professional assistance available?" asked Kyle.

"Absolutely," said James as he began to get teary eyed.

"Are you willing to forget about your kidnapping and subsequent interrogation?" asked Kyle.

"Without a doubt. I can fix it so none of this ever happened," said James as he finally broke down and started crying.

"One final question," said Kenny. "Do you know the name of the group your brother was affiliated with?" asked Kenny.

"Armageddon," said Detective James. The Rhobertses looked at each other and Fuentes and thought they were finally getting somewhere.

Kenny kneeled down in front of James for effect, gave a very intense stare and asked, "Did you cry when Old Yeller died, James?" James looked very confused and continued to look at Kenny. Fuentes turned around quickly to hide his smile. Kyle just shook his head in disbelief and thought they had all just lost all credibility.

Chapter 27

The Rhobertses released Detective James from the chair and showed him a place where he could clean up. Fuentes stood guard outside the large restroom that Detective James was using. When James finished, Fuentes escorted him to a large conference room. The large table within the room was rectangular and made of the finest wood that James had ever seen. The pattern of the wood grain was so beautiful; it reminded Detective James of a grade six shotgun stock he had seen once at a skeet range in Dallas. Imagine the wood stain stock, but on a very large table surrounded by twelve chairs. In front of each chair, a laptop computer sat with full access to the internet. The computers were custom made by Suzy Rhoberts and had 200 GB memory and a Pentium 8 processor that was not yet available to the public. The Rhobertses were at the far end of the table with their sister watching as Fuentes escorted Detective James in to the room. Five of the twelve computers were up and running.

"Have a seat over at that terminal," said Kenny as he motioned to the chair next to Suzy.

"We have it connected for you," said Suzy.

"Thank you. And I'm sorry about grabbing you the way I did earlier. I hope I didn't hurt you?" said James.

"See those two," said Suzy while motioning to her brothers. "They have done a lot worse than you. I hesitate to bring it up, as it shames me so, but those are my brothers."

"We tried to kill her several times, but Mom just wouldn't have it," said Kenny.

"I'll give you some credit, James," said Kyle who wasn't into small talk with those he didn't quite trust yet, "you made some very interesting observations of our work at the crime scenes."

"I'm a homicide detective and I've been doing this kind of work for a while. I have a few questions of my own, if you don't mind," said James.

"In just a minute. First, I want to know how you are going to explain your disappearance to your supervisors in Dallas without causing suspicion or your termination," said Kyle.

"I've been thinking about that," said James. "We were in the back of the restaurant when the abduction took place. There could only have been a very few who witnessed the incident. I'll call my supervisors in a minute and check in as if nothing has happened. When asked about what happened, the few, or the one that witnessed the abduction will have to have made a formal statement by now. I was going to tell them that they were mistaken and that I took the lovely lady I was eating lunch with back to her place." Looking at Suzy now, James said, "I certainly wouldn't want to sully your reputation or make it seem that you are so easy, but it's the best I can come up with."

"I'm not offended, Detective. Please continue," said Suzy.

"Well, as I didn't want to be disturbed, I turned my pager off. I'm not a ladies man, per se, and I don't think my deputy chief will make too much of a deal about it when explained to him," said James. "As far as the chase is concerned, I was going to mention the fact that some of the people we get into chase with will run just for having a simple warrant out for a traffic violation. Or, that it could have been some kind of fraternity prank."

"A fraternity prank? A high-speed chase with suspects who have access to stop sticks and disappeared?" said Kyle with doubt on his mind.

"Hey, you're forgetting something," said James. "I don't know anything about any chase. I was getting busy with a beautiful girl that I met for lunch," said James and he couldn't look at Suzy this time.

"What about the lapse in time from your lunch to now? How are you going to explain that?" asked Kenny.

"I was going to say that I hadn't taken much time off in my entire career and that I was going to tell my supervisor the next day. I didn't think it would be that big of a problem," said James. A long pause while everyone in the room was considering the detective's story.

"If you think it'll work, then I guess you can try it," said Kyle.

"You had better make the call soon, though. The longer you take in telling your story, the weaker it gets," said Kenny.

"I can use my cell phone if you guys still have it. That way, they won't know where I'm at," said James.

"Unless they check and find out which cell tower is broadcasting your signal," said Suzy.

"They won't. That takes too much paperwork and if I'm talking to them and telling them I'm fine, they won't bother," said James.

"Then make it happen. You will understand if we listen in to the conversation ourselves? Trust has to be earned, you know," said Kyle.

"I understand. Moreover, yes, I know trust has to be earned. In my occupation, you trust no one. That's how you stay alive," said James.

"Not just in your occupation, my friend," said Kenny.

"Can I ask those questions now?" asked James.

"Let's see how the phone call makes out and then we'll talk," said Kyle.

"Fair enough," said James.

"*The Right Stuff*," said Kenny.

"Excuse me?" said James.

"Just before breaking the sound barrier in the movie *The Right Stuff*, Chuck Yaeger asks his pilot buddy for a piece of Beemans Gum. Yaeger tells him that he'll pay him back later and his friend says, 'Fair enough'," said Kenny.

"I forgot that one," said Fuentes.

"I remember it but it hardly seems relevant," said Kyle.

"Remember when you said your brother was a bit of a nut?" asked Suzy to Detective James.

"Yeah," said James.

"Well my brothers are nuts themselves. Always quoting movies at the most inappropriate times," said Suzy.

"Frankly, my dear, I don't give a damn," said Kenny.

"See what I mean?" as Suzy motioned to Kenny. Detective James was beginning to wonder what he got himself into. Were these the same guys who were killing murderers and known offenders in Dallas?

Detective James made the phone call in the presence of the Rhobertses and Fuentes. It seemed by the end of the conversation that he had his chief convinced that the witnesses at the incident were mistaken. He also managed a request to take a few weeks off. Detective James had a way with persuading his superiors. "What's our next move?" asked James.

"Simple," said Kyle. "We go to this ranch that you've seen in McKinney and do some surveillance. We need to follow a few of the members and get to know them. In a friendly manner, we need to convince some of them that we hate illegal immigrants or Yankees or whatever it is they want to hear," said Kyle.

"That sounds like an excellent plan," said James.

"An excellent plan that can get us all killed," said Kenny. "There are no perfect plans, just tactics that may or may not work," said Kenny which caused confusion in the room.

"I don't know that one. Which movie is that from?" asked Fuentes.

"None," said Kenny, "I just made it up."

Chapter 28

"Let's talk about this plan of yours, Kenny," said John Rhoberts who arrived after hearing the news of Detective James.

"I hadn't really had time to put anything together, Dad," said Kenny. "Kyle and I were talking about this a while ago. If they are as extreme as it appears, then getting in close enough to find out valuable information could take years. On the other hand, if we can find a member who secludes himself for a short period of time, maybe we can interrogate him."

"Worked on me," said Detective James.

"You actually did better than most," said Kyle to James. James had a brief smile on his face and he turned his face the other direction.

"If you go the kidnapping and interrogation route this time, could you do us all the courtesy of staying off the news this time?" said John Rhoberts.

"It was Kyle's pathetic driving, Dad," said Kenny.

"I didn't think it would take you five minutes to subdue a man that had already been restrained by your sister," snapped Kyle. Fuentes was smiling because he knew what was happening this time. Detective James looked confused believing he was watching a problem about to explode. But James saw the look on Fuentes' face. It looked as if he were enjoying a movie or something.

"See what you started, Dad? Now we'll never get anything accomplished," said Suzy, very carefully to her father.

"All right, that's enough," said John Rhoberts as he stood. Everyone in the room got quiet. John Rhoberts had that effect on people. He began to pace the large living room that was artificially illuminated with mercury lights. His footsteps echoed off the walls from the dark hardwood floors. Four soft, dark brown, leather couches were placed facing each other as if you were in an intersection with four stop signs. "You need to find the local hangout for these guys. Preferably one in which they serve alcohol. Watch them for a few weeks if you need that long. Find the weak link. There is always at least one that just cannot keep his mouth shut. Do not question him there. I say this for your benefit, Kenny," said John Rhoberts.

"Hey! I know better than that," said Kenny.

"Shall I tell Fuentes and James about the incident in Las Vegas?" asked John Rhoberts. Kenny's face changed and turned the brightest pink you have ever seen.

"Let's move on, Dad," said Kenny with his head low.

Suzy and Kyle were laughing across the room and Kyle said, "Didn't you tell that guy at the bar that he had a nice ass?" And Suzy fell off the couch that she was sitting on and was holding her stomach telling Kyle to stop.

"Shut up, Kyle. We have stories about you too, Mr. Man," said Kenny.

"All right, enough. I shouldn't have brought it up. Getting back to the point," said John Rhoberts as he was watching Kenny flip off his sister because she was still laughing. "All I'm saying is that y'all find one that you don't necessarily think will be missed. That way, you don't raise suspicion if he doesn't return." And as he finished that sentence, John Rhoberts looked at Detective James for any sign of discomfort or hesitation. Everyone in the room would follow suit.

"Hey, these guys killed my brother and God knows how many other innocents. Don't worry about me. I'm in," said Detective James.

"From a distance. Since your brother was killed by this group for ratting them out, that takes you off the surveillance team. No one can see you in the area or you could blow the whole thing. We may have already sent up a red flag with your capture the other day," said Kyle.

"But I need to show you guys where the ranch is and…" started Detective James until Kyle cut him off.

"We appreciate what you want to do for your brother. I promise you, you will get a chance to avenge your brother. And I think we can find the ranch with your assistance, but you cannot interact with these people. There is too much at risk," said Kyle.

"Fair enough," said James.

"You can help me with taking pictures of the ones that get close enough to the van and get positive identification for us," said Suzy. "And Fuentes can put taps on the phone lines from the street box."

"Yeah, I guess Fuentes would pass for a local phone guy, if he gained about a hundred pounds and wore baggy jeans and showed his butt," said Kenny.

"Well, you would know all about male butts, wouldn't you, Kenny?" said a laughing Kyle. The room was temporarily roaring with laughter.

Suzy's face turned red and said, "I would have to agree with you on one point, Kenny. That guy at the bar in Vegas did have a nice ass."

Kenny quickly looked at Fuentes and James and said, "I had a few rum and Cokes and the guy's hair was long and very blonde and…"

"It's pathetic that you should feel the need to explain yourself, son," said John Rhoberts.

"It was an honest mistake. They only do this to you because you do it to them. And you must admit, it was kind of funny," said Fuentes.

"Why don't you all go and cram it up your cram-holes," said Kenny as he stormed out of the room.

"I know that one," said Fuentes who was stifling his laughter. "That's from the movie *Dodgeball*."

Chapter 29

Sergeant Fuentes called Colonel Smith and gave him an update on everything they learned from Detective James. "Why is it that the police always have more information than we do?" asked the colonel who seemed a bit frustrated.

"My guess, Colonel, would be that the police are on the streets 24/7 and our intelligence guys aren't," said Fuentes.

"That's a safe assessment, Sergeant. Anything you need from me?" asked the colonel.

"We might need some additional surveillance gear, Colonel. From what Detective James was telling us, this ranch will be a little difficult to monitor," said Fuentes.

"Have the Rhobertses advise you on the materials they need and I'll see to it that they get it," said the colonel.

"Yes sir. Will that be all, Colonel?" asked Fuentes.

"One more thing, Sergeant. How do you feel about Detective James? That is, do you trust the information he provided?" asked Colonel Smith.

"Under the circumstances, yeah, I believe every word," said Fuentes.

"Good. That will be all, Sergeant," and the colonel hung up the phone.

"Same attitude, different day. He needs to lighten up a little," thought Sergeant Fuentes.

"I know what you're thinking, son," said John Rhoberts who was standing behind Fuentes. The sergeant was caught off guard a little. He didn't hear Mr. Rhoberts approach. "But Sheldon Smith has always been like that. Even to his friends. He is not one to dawdle on the phone. He says what he needs to and gets off the phone or simply walks away from you. It takes some getting used to, but eventually you figure out that it's just the way he is. Don't take it personally."

"I try not to, sir," said Fuentes.

"Good. Let's get you guys packed for the trip, get an aerial of the ranch and try to figure out what kind of equipment y'all are going to need," said John Rhoberts who then slapped Fuentes on the back.

Fuentes thought, "Ouch," but certainly didn't say it.

"This would be a lot easier if we had more intel," said Suzy.

"You remember those high-powered cameras the networks were using to film the debacle in Waco a few years back?" asked Kyle.

"Yeah, but those are the networks. Those cameras are as big as big as a telephone booth. What's your point?" replied Suzy.

"Camera lenses and computer chips have come a long way in the last few years," said Kyle.

"You're not going to spill out a bunch of those stupid marbles are you?" asked Suzy.

"Hey! Those stupid marbles are made by me, so let's not talk about my marbles," said Kenny.

"It would be so easy to say something right now," said Kyle with a grin.

"You left yourself wide open for that one," said Detective James.

"What are you talking about, Dick James?" said Kenny with a bit of nasty sarcasm. "It took you four different crime scenes before you even found a marble camera."

"Well, to be honest, I didn't figure it out. Our best crime scene detective Drew Michaels figured it out," said Detective James.

"And how did he do that? We know Drew Michaels and I never once saw him pick up one of my cameras," said Kenny.

"Well, he said he could pick up a low-level signal from each of the crime scenes. The signal was scrambled and low frequency as I mentioned before, and Drew said that with our limited technology on the department, he would never find the source. He thought if he had access and training on better tracking devices, he might actually have a shot. And the only common denominator at each crime scene was a single marble," said James.

"Impressive. But why didn't he take one to examine it further?" asked Kenny.

"Because he thinks like a cop. If there is still a signal coming from the marble, or camera, he didn't want to let on that he was wise to it. He told me about his suspicions and I began to pick them up. It was more out of frustration than gathering evidence. You guys have eluded us for so long now, I just wanted some way of telling you I knew something," said James.

"So how well do you know Drew Michaels?" asked Kyle?

"Pretty well. He's a good officer and takes his job very seriously. We don't have Thanksgiving and Christmas together, if that's what you mean. Why?" asked James.

"I just thought at some point in time, it would be useful to have a cleaner," said Kyle.

"A cleaner? What do we need a cleaner for?" asked Kenny.

"You never know, Kenny. Aren't you tired of being watched or chased by the authorities?" asked Kyle.

"Cleaning the scenes won't stop that, Kyle," said Kenny.

"He's right. It will only fuel the frustration in the police department," said James, "Besides, I'm pretty sure that Drew wouldn't be interested in changing sides." Kenny, Kyle, Suzy and Fuentes all turned to look at Detective James. John Rhoberts was in the room but pretended not to hear it. This was a matter of discussion between the kids, he thought.

"What do you mean by switching sides? Do you mean to say that in the police department's eyes, we are the bad guys?" asked Kenny.

"Not at all," said James, "and don't take offense, because it wasn't meant that way. Drew has been insistent on being in on your crime scenes because he felt, as I did, that we were dealing with professionals. He simply doesn't trust anyone else to do it. Furthermore, after searching all your crime scenes and gathering what little information we could get from eyewitnesses, he would be disappointed, like I was, to find out that you two were just men. I'm not into flattery and I am not blowing smoke up your butts. It's just when you have researched, and studied, and gone to witnesses' homes time after time to find something, anything that you've missed, it's frustrating. Therefore, what I meant by switching sides was that he won't give up on finding you two. I wasn't going to give up on you either, until I truly knew you guys."

"Do you truly know us, Detective James?" asked Kyle.

"I believe I do, yes. I have spoken with you, your family members and Sergeant Fuentes and I'll try and say this without being corny, but I sense no evil here. I believe your intentions were pure at each crime scene and so do many other officers. However, due to the nature of the law, we must find those who take the law in to their own hands and bring them before the courts. Even if we believe that what they're doing is the right thing," said Detective James.

"Therein lies the problem with the law," said Kenny.

"So who says that Detectives Jesse James and Drew Michaels aren't going to get their men?" said Kyle. Kenny raised his hand quickly as if in a classroom and he was dying to tell everyone the answer. Detective James wore a very confused look on his face. Kyle laughed at Kenny and said, "Don't you tell them, Kenny. Not yet."

Kenny's face grimaced and said, "I never get to do anything."

Chapter 30

The Rhobertses finished packing the Hummer and one of their utility trucks. "Did you get the AT&T magnetic signs for the doors?" asked Kyle.

"Yeah, I got the CoServ magnetic signs too, in case we do the power trick on them," said Kenny, "I also put a couple of Water Utilities signs and Baby on Board signs in the back of the truck. You know, for the hell of it."

"Won't they know we have a baby on board when they see you?" asked Kyle with a smile.

"Hardy, har, har. Why don't you go and milk a cat," said Kenny.

"I am getting kind of hungry," said Kyle, "not that cat milk sounds good." Then Kyle looked on his wrist at the Timex Iron Man watch and it clearly said Thursday. "Thursday," said Kyle aloud, so his brother could hear it.

"Thursday? Oh, Yeah! All you can eat catfish at Dreams on the Bayou on Thursday nights. Good call," said Kenny. Dreams on the Bayou was a local restaurant at Lake Bistineau that the Rhobertses loved. The Rhobertses extended the invitation to everyone in the house as long as they kept a somewhat low profile. As soon as the brothers mentioned the restaurant, everyone went to the bathrooms to see how they looked.

"You have to look good for all you can eat catfish?" asked Kenny to his mother and sister.

"I have to look good wherever I go, Kenny," said Suzy.

"Then I suggest that you not go out at all," said Kenny in a run as his sister followed close behind. "Mom, Suzy is running in the house," yelled Kenny. John Rhoberts left the house with Fuentes and Detective James.

"They'll be another hour screwing around and I'm hungry. Y'all coming? First beer is on me," said John Rhoberts.

"Right behind you, sir," said Fuentes.

"Yeah, I'm coming," said Detective James. "Is Kenny ever serious?"

"It's rare, but yeah, he can be serious," said their father.

Dreams on the Bayou was a quaint, quiet spot to have some really good catfish and steaks. The restaurant was family owned and they were very friendly. The décor in the place was entirely lake house. Fishing poles, fishing motors, canoes, lures, pirogues and of course, fish. The restaurant itself was on the second floor of a two-story wooden structure. It was called it a structure because no one exactly knew how they managed to build it. Or what building plans, if any, were used to help construct it. There was plenty of room in the dining area for guests with a small salad bar in the corner. The windows all along the southern wall were facing Lake Bistineau and as far as you could see, there were moss-covered trees.

"Oh, I love to hear the bullfrogs," said Suzy as she approached the stairs to the restaurant. Bullfrogs were croaking in twenty or thirty different spots from what Fuentes could tell.

"You, uh. You love to hear the bullfrogs?" asked Fuentes.

"Yeah. It's kind of relaxing, don't you think?" asked Suzy.

"I never really thought about it," said Fuentes.

"Big surprise, there," said Suzy as she rolled her eyes. "The only thing Kenny or Kyle could tell you about bullfrogs is how they taste or the fact that they get quiet when someone approaches. They don't listen to them at all. It's just not a guy thing," Suzy said to her mother, Barbara.

"I don't get the whole bullfrog thing myself, honey, but it doesn't mean it isn't important to you," said Barbara Rhoberts.

Kenny smiled and said, "Did you get that? No one understands the bullfrogs but you. Hence you are a..."

"That's enough, Kenny. Go upstairs and make sure your father isn't getting mad at the wait staff," said Barbara.

"Yes, ma'am," said Kenny as he flipped off his sister behind his mother's back. Suzy smiled and stuck her tongue out at Kenny. Kenny yelled back at her as he ran upstairs, "No thanks, I use toilet paper."

"God, Mom. Is he ever going to grow up? And if he starts on any of those stupid kid jokes with Kyle, well, I'm leaving," said Suzy.

"It's nice to have the family under one roof, don't you think?" said Barbara with a note of sarcasm.

Suzy smiled, "I guess so. No, yeah, it is. I just think Kenny shouldn't be allowed to have any caffeine or sugar in his diet."

"We all agree on that, honey," said Barbara Rhoberts.

Dinner went well and everyone was headed back to the house. Suzy gathered some of her things and told them she would see them tomorrow. John and Barbara Rhoberts left just after Suzy because John didn't like to sleep anywhere but his own bed. Kenny and Fuentes took turns playing games and searching the sky in the chair until early morning. Kyle turned in and told Detective James he was welcome to use the house as he needed. Detective James took the only other available bedroom. He was full of catfish, hush puppies, and beer (and not in that order). By the time he washed up, he was about to just climb on the bed and sleep but someone had been in the room. There were a pair of men's Superman pajama pants and a t-shirt laid over the bed with new tags on them.

"Thanks, Kenny," said James more to himself than Kenny.

"You're welcome," said Kenny from the closet and he opened the door and walked out of the room as if he was just passing through.

"Who are these guys?" thought Detective James. "Professional, yet so weird. Knowledgeable, yet so confusing. Compassionate, yet so infuriating. Sleep. I need sleep." And the house went quiet until morning.

Chapter 31

Detective James was slowly waking up and felt someone in the room. James sat up in bed and gave a loud stretch and said, "Good morning, Kenny," to the closet.

A long pause in the room until, "Dang it," and Kenny once again opened the closet and came out. "Only because I wanted you to hear me," said Kenny as he walked out of the room. "Hurry up and get vertical. We're watching *Super Troopers* and they are about to chug the syrup. I love it when they get all antsy in their pantsy," said Kenny. Fuentes was in the chair playing a flight simulator game while Kenny and Kyle made some scrambled eggs and bacon.

"Some amateurs add milk in their omelet for density; this is a mistake," said Kenny.

"That's from the movie *Deep Blue Sea*," said Fuentes.

"He's getting pretty good at this," said Kyle.

"Good at what?" asked Detective James as he entered the room.

"Oh, no you don't. You do not just walk into a room and ask a question about the conversation. It makes people feel like they have to start from the beginning of the conversation to appease you. And at seven in the morning, I'm not about appeasing anyone," said Kyle.

"You'll have to forgive Kyle, Jesse. He's not a morning person and he hasn't killed anyone in a week," said Kenny with a show of concern on his face.

"No big deal. So what's the plan?" asked James.

"Well, we eat breakfast. We pack the equipment we need for this excursion into the Humvee and we take off for the ranch in McKinney. I thought Kenny and Fuentes could take the utility truck while you and I take the Hummer," said Kyle to Detective James.

"Sounds great," said James, "Have you had any sugar today, Kenny?"

"Why does everyone always ask me that? Yeah, I had a couple of Cokes. So what?" asked Kenny?

"So you haven't sat down since you got up," said Fuentes as he was trying to land a plane at Love Field Airport on the simulator.

"Do you want your eggs runny? Do ya, Fermentes?" asked Kenny. "You like airplane food, boy?"

"It's not working. I can see that you're trying to distract me from my textbook landing. Jealousy is so ugly," said Fuentes. Kyle knew what Kenny was about to do. Kenny took a remote from a drawer in the kitchen and changed the altimeter in the flight simulator. Fuentes' plane dropped five hundred feet in a second and he was in a stall.

"What the hell happened?" yelled Fuentes.

"I don't know. Were you watching the artificial horizon?" asked Kenny.

"I'll tell you what happened. You were getting close to Kenny's high score and the floor bottomed out on you," said Kyle.

"You cheated me of my perfect score because I was going to break your record?" asked Fuentes.

"No. I messed with your flight because you were talking smack about me being hyper. I hope you can explain to all the people on that flight as to why you were distracted from landing the airplane. In addition, all their families because you had to smack on Daddy.

Shame," said Kenny as the window screen was showing a massive explosion.

"I don't think you used that street terminology correctly," said Detective James.

"Just for that, my good man, there will be no gratuity," said Kenny as he made himself a plate of scrambled eggs, four strips of lean bacon and a small bowl of grits. Fuentes was being lowered in the chair as the game was over and thinking about the quote from Kenny.

"I don't know that one," said Fuentes while approaching the kitchen.

"It's from a Warner Brothers cartoon. Daffy Duck says it," said Kyle. "Cracks me up every time too. Eat already. We are not staying here all day. We have to go over there and fix the place up tonight. Once we get Suzy hooked up for sight and sound, we can just find a hole and watch the show for a while."

"Is she coming then?" asked James.

"She's probably already on the way. She wanted to scout some properties that were close to the ranch so we could set up a lab and observation room," said Kyle.

"We just have to be sure there are no restrictions on the property. We might have to do with a trailer for a while, but as far as I can tell, neither one of you are strangers to homes on wheels," said Kenny. "I'm sorry. That wasn't politically correct, was it?" said Kenny as he raised both hands to make explanation marks in the air. "They're called 'manufactured homes' now."

"What have you got against trailers…uh, manufactured homes? I know a lot of good people who live in them," said James.

"Boom! There you go," said Kenny. "Nothing! I have absolutely nothing against the people living in the homes. But I like where this discussion is going so please continue," said Kenny.

"Look, as long as people are happy living in them, what's the difference?" asked James.

"Nothing. Stop talking about the people in the homes. I hate that some people cannot afford a home that's attached to the ground, not just connected to it. I hate that some of the manufactured homes builders have used cheap construction materials to keep down costs. I hate being delayed on the highway because they have blocked all lanes with half of a manufactured home. But most of all, I hate it when you see news coverage of a bad thunderstorm or tornado, and all you could see are torn up manufactured homes and clothes. No, I am not insulting anyone who has ever lived in a trailer because we have lived in one. I simply think of them as deathtraps and feel sorry for anyone inside them," said Kenny.

"I do love it when someone says something and another person hears something else. I failed sensitivity training. I don't hate being misunderstood, mind you. I get that a lot. I dislike it when the retort from the individual is ladled out with sarcasm when it didn't need to be. You could have simply said, 'What do you mean by that?' and I would have explained. No smart remark needed," said Kenny.

"We're getting a little off the point here, aren't we?" said Kyle with a grin. "I swear, Kenny. You did fail sensitivity training. Passionate much?"

"Shut up, Wilson," said Kenny to Kyle.

"*Castaway*," said Fuentes and James at the same time.

Chapter 32

"I didn't mean to get Kenny all riled up this morning," said Detective James to Kyle. They were about an hour west of Shreveport on Interstate 20.

"You didn't rile him. He doesn't like it when anyone insinuates that he might be prejudiced to a social class or race or gender or whatever," said Kyle.

"That's not what I said. I didn't insinuate that at all," said James.

"Didn't you hear him? Didn't you get it? He said it's not what you say; it's when you hear what he said the wrong way and then speak on it without confirming your doubts," said Kyle.

"I'm getting a headache," said James.

"Me too. Have a Coke and a smile," said Kyle as he handed James a coke from a cooler at his feet. "I took these from Kenny's truck, so enjoy."

"O.K., now this time I'm going to be Noah, of Noah's Ark, and who are you going to be?" asked Kenny to Fuentes.

"I'm going to be, uh, Shaggy from Scooby Doo," said Fuentes.

"O.K., go." said Kenny.

"Hey, like how's it hangin', Noah? Seen any ghosts?" asked Fuentes.

"What the hell is wrong with you, boy? Don't you know you are about to be swimming in the greatest tempest of all time? You see me packing the animals two at a time, dontcha," said Kenny, "and when I say packing, I don't mean, 'packin'.'"

"Zoinks! Is it going to be like a real flood, man? Oh, man. I just got hungry too. Like, take me to the kitchen, Noah, and let's scarf some grimace proportions, dude," said Fuentes.

"All right! Enough with the Shaggy impersonator. The surfer thing wears on me pretty quick," said Kenny. "Wait. I got it. I got it. This will be a good one. You can be Jennifer Aniston and I'll be Angelina Jolie," said Kenny.

"Man, I wish. I would spend hours in front of the mirror, but anyway, sounds fun! Let's do it. You go first," said Fuentes.

"O.K.," a long pause and then, "Bitch!" said Kenny with an evil grin.

"Press whore," spat Fuentes. Kenny chuckled at that one.

"Your show *Friends* sucked," said Kenny to a now laughing Fuentes.

"Humanitarian hag," said Fuentes as he could barely say it without laughing.

Kenny swerved in the road he was laughing so hard, but somehow, he managed to yell out, "Hollywood harlot." Kyle and Detective James pulled up next to Kenny and Fuentes and watched them red faced and laughing in the cab of the utility truck.

"I bet they're talking about doo-doo," said Kyle. Kyle motioned at Kenny to roll down his window. Kenny rolled it down and the laughter was seeping out of the car. "Hey, guys. Want to keep it together or what?" asked Kyle. Kenny got worse and grabbed his stomach.

"Keep it together! Keep them together! It's too late for that," laughed Kenny.

"You two need a break. Let's stop at the next rest area and have a chat," said Kyle.

"O.K., if we can keep it together," said Kenny still chuckling.

"I swear that boy doesn't have a serious bone in his body. Now don't get me wrong," said Kyle as he rolled his window back up, "there is no one better in a hot spot than Kenny. It's just, sometimes, he doesn't know when to stop being a kid," said Kyle a little annoyed.

"Yeah, I miss him too," said James.

"I didn't say I missed him," said Kyle.

"But that's what I heard you say," said James.

"Touché," said Kyle.

"He really is something to watch. Always entertaining and on the move," said James.

"Yeah, he's all right," said Kyle. "Sometimes!"

Chapter 33

Kyle's cell phone was ringing. It was Suzy.

"She has already found us a property to lease and has a trailer already on it. Electricity and phone lines are being put in as we speak. According to Suzy, it's somewhere just west of Interstate 75 and north of Highway 380. Know where that is?" asked Kyle.

"I know exactly where that is. That only puts us several miles away from the ranch," said Detective James rubbing his hands together.

"Getting nervous?" asked Kyle.

"Not nervous. Anxious. I have been waiting a long time for something like this to happen. I have always known that my brother was murdered and I haven't been able to escape the realism that I couldn't do anything about it alone. Not against an adversary like this one," said Jesse.

"I'm curious as to what action you think we are actually going to take out here, Jesse. Besides the obvious observation and interrogation," said Kyle.

"Well, I'm not really sure. I assume that since these people have somehow or another targeted your family, you will target them. Y'all have a close family. I have rarely seen such loyalty in a family. It's becoming obsolete," said Jesse.

"Not so obsolete that we don't see it in you, Jesse. We know about your brother and what that must have felt like. To have that on your mind for so long must have been torture. Even though your brother may have strayed off the path, you still want to avenge him, right? Was it because you saw your brother in memories of how you guys used to be? Memories of changing your little brother's diapers or chasing him down when he crawls off with the remote? Or was it that you saw your brother every time you look in the mirror? I'm sorry. I ramble on like that from time to time. Just thinking aloud. You don't have to answer those," said Kyle.

"No, I don't mind. It's actually nice to talk about it. I've kept it bottled up inside for so long now. It's amazing I'm not on Prozac or something. To answer the questions, I would simply say that it was a combination of all of those that make it hurt. Being a police officer kind of relieves the stress, you know. Something about the adrenaline in catching the bad guy or figuring out what the suspect was thinking when he did it. Takes me away from the jagged truth and murder of my brother," said Jesse. An uncomfortable silence prevailed in the Hummer for a little while until the rest area stop was a mile away.

"Thank goodness. I need a stretch and I haven't had a run all week," said Kyle.

"I know what you mean. I'm still hurting from the catfish and beer," said Jesse with a small grin.

"Bet it hurt to say that," said Kyle.

"Not as bad as you might think. Cops are not always drinkers like those that they make out in the movies. I can normally hold my own, but I was celebrating last night, in a sense," said Jesse.

"I saw that. We're glad to help you out on this one, Jesse. I hope when this is all over, everyone is satisfied," said Kyle.

"I'm sure we will be. Or we'll be dead," said Jesse. Kenny pulled up next to Kyle and motioned Jesse to roll down his window. Jesse rolled down his window and motioned towards the rest area sign.

Kenny said, "Are you pulling me over? Is this a traffic stop, Officer? What's your probable cause? You have not read me my Miranda Rights! This is police harassment! You just hate me because I am Middle-Eastern!…Did I miss any?" asked Kenny.

"I think you got most of them," said Jesse.

They pulled over at the rest stop and everyone had a pee break. They all went to the soda machines because that was where Kenny ended up anyway. Kyle told them about what Suzy had accomplished and called her for better directions to the trailer.

"Are we going to be on-line tonight? Great job, Sis. We'll see you in a bit," said Kyle. "She is going to have everything ready when we get there. We just have to do the sight and sound. In addition, with a group like this, we had better take it slow. We cannot raise any alarms putting up the surveillance equipment. Everybody get your game faces on," said Kyle to Kenny. "That goes double for you."

"What?" said Kenny as he took a third Dr. Pepper out of the machine. "Lord knows when we'll be next to a soda machine again. Does she have a refrigerator ready and fully stocked?" asked Kenny to Kyle.

"I forgot to ask. Why don't you call her and find out if we need to pick up some supplies," said Kyle.

"I'll take care of it. I need the local phone pole numbers as they relate to the ranch and their locations as well as the closest power line to the ranch that is off property. She probably already has it done, but it would expedite things to know it's done," said Kenny.

"See? Get him talking about the job at hand and he's all professional," whispered Kyle to Jesse.

"I'm sorry, Jesse, I didn't see any donuts in the machines," said Kenny. Kyle looked a little disappointed at the remark. "What?" asked Kenny. "What?"

Chapter 34

The Rhobertses arrived at the trailer a little after 7:00 P.M. Suzy was waiting at the trailer with the door open. "I just finished putting up the satellite link. I had a land line put in just in case, but most of that was for show," said Suzy.

"For show?" asked Jesse.

"Yeah. We don't use land lines much with the satellite hook-ups, but if anyone was paying attention to the move-in, it would have looked odd not to have a land line," said Kyle.

"Makes sense," said Fuentes.

"Have you got the plans I asked for, Suzy?" asked Kenny.

"Yeah. And I already took care of the power line that was hooked up to their compound," said Suzy.

"How did you manage that? I mean, without suspicion?" asked Kenny.

"I'm not without contacts, Kenny, as you well know. All you need to know is we're hooked in. The phone box you need to work on is located at grid 118 columns C, D and E on this map," said Suzy pointing to a map on the table. "It shouldn't be that difficult to hook up, but it is close to the compound."

"I'll get suited up for that with Fuentes. Let's go, Sergeant," said Kenny.

"While you guys are doing that, I'm going for a jog," said Kyle.

"A jog? Now?" asked Jesse.

"He's going to run the outside perimeter of the ranch and check for entry and exit points. You know, find the weak spots in the armor," said Suzy.

"Oh. Well what do I do?" asked Jesse.

"Sit tight with me. I may need you to help me gain access to your police department's files on fingerprints and suspect identification," said Suzy.

"Kinda boring compared to what the others are doing, don't you think?" asked Jesse.

"That's the job," said Suzy.

Kenny put the magnetic phone signs on the utility truck and put on his jumpsuit. "I got you one too," said Kenny to Fuentes.

"The name on my suit is Roy," said Fuentes.

"I know. Kind of cool, huh? Mine is Bubba. Just a couple of country boys working for the phone company. I regret that I could not find suits that showed our butt cracks. Those were all sold out," said Kenny. Kenny and Fuentes found the phone box labeled on the map. Kenny parked the truck on the shoulder of the road and put out several traffic cones for effect. Kenny had just gained access to the box when a McKinney police squad car pulled up next to them.

"What's up?" said the officer to Kenny and Fuentes.

"Just a maintenance check on the box. Checking for corrosion and making sure we have a solid line," said Kenny.

"Where's Austin?" asked the officer. "Isn't this his area?"

"Yeah. He has a case of the trots, so I told him I'd take his maintenance checks today," said Kenny.

"A case of the trots, huh? Does your buddy talk, or what?" said the officer motioning towards Fuentes.

"He doesn't habla English," said Kenny. This seemed to infuriate the officer. His face changed at once and he got out of his vehicle.

"What do you mean, he doesn't habla English?" asked the officer approaching Fuentes with a tone of disapproval. "He's working for an American phone company in Texas, and they don't think he needs to habla English?" said the officer.

"We have a lot of customers that are Hispanic and I don't speak Spanish. What's the big deal?" said Kenny.

"The big deal is, he took the job of an English-speaking, red, white and blue American. In addition, because he is probably here illegally, the phone company can pay him the very minimum amount to save money. It's a system that's tearing this country apart," said the officer.

"I don't really see why this is any concern of yours, Officer. We just came out to check this box and we are gone. Is that a problem?" asked Kenny approaching the officer.

"Where is your phone company identification? Let me see it," asked the officer.

"I'm not required to show you my phone identification. If you would like to see my driver's license you can," said Kenny now face to face with the officer.

"How about your work orders for the day?" asked the officer.

"I told you this was a maintenance check. There aren't any work orders for routine maintenance," said Kenny as he spit to the side of the officer. Kenny waited while the officer considered the information. Fuentes was backing up towards the utility truck in case this went bad and he needed a weapon.

"Next time, don't bring any foreigners to maintain our phone lines. In fact, only Austin is supposed to be maintaining this area. I don't want to see you two around here again," said the officer.

"Well, we'll certainly pass on the message. I don't know why anyone wouldn't want to come out here, though. The hospitality is overwhelming," said Kenny.

"Don't push it, smartass," snapped the officer. Kenny did not respond. He simply turned around and went back to the phone box. The McKinney police officer left but only after staring at Fuentes for a good sixty seconds.

"Gee, ya think he might be oppressed in some way?" asked Fuentes.

"What I figure about that guy is that he's on the ranch's payroll. It was when he said 'our phone lines.' We may have been made. If he calls this in to the phone company, they won't have any record of our doing maintenance out here tonight," said Kenny.

"Can't we get Suzy to tap into their records and add the work order to the computer?" asked Fuentes.

"Not after the fact. Most of the entries are time coded. Probably for some kind of customer satisfaction survey or something. Besides, he saw our nametags on our jumpsuits. All he has to do is call his contact at the phone company and find out if Bubba and Roy work the phone company in this area," said Kenny.

"Yeah. Question is, how many Bubbas and Roys are they going to have to ask before they figure out it wasn't their guys?" said Fuentes.

"It doesn't matter anymore. I'm finished. The phone lines are tagged. Let's blow this pop stand. I might like to get a heads-up to Kyle while he's doing the perimeter check. Let him know they have the cops in their pockets. Or at least one of them," said Kenny.

"How are you going to do that? Did he take a radio?" asked Fuentes.

"Nope. Scrambled satellite phone," said Kenny. "I made one that looks like a walkman."

Chapter 35

"They have dogs in the perimeter," said Kyle when he got back to the trailer.

"What kind of dogs?" asked Kenny.

"The best trained German shepherds I have seen in a long time," said Kyle.

"What makes you say that?" asked Jesse.

"They only bark to notify the owners of your presence while you're in their area. When you are out of range, the next dog picks up your scent, and the other goes back to his post. Nothing personal. All business. That's high-dollar training," said Kyle.

"And the angles? Did they cover optimum angles?" asked Kenny.

"Yeah. They had all the angles covered. I'm telling you, they were good," said Kyle.

"There's only a couple of guys we know of who can train dogs like that. However, let's not waste our time on that. Fuentes, call the colonel and see what he can dig up on the dog trainers. He knows who to check. Tell him we want to know who bought twenty shepherds at top dollar. The colonel shouldn't mind making a little inquiry about the dogs. After all, he's still commander of the military police on base isn't he," asked Kenny.

"Yes, sir, he is," said Fuentes.

"Good deal. He would be less likely to raise an eyebrow if someone were paying close attention," said Kenny.

"We're going to need some dog treats," said Kyle.

"Wait. If these dogs are so highly trained, how can you distract them with dog treats?" asked Jesse.

"By dog treats, I didn't mean milk bones. I meant some tranquilizers from our air pistols," said Kyle.

"Are we planning on getting that close?" asked Kenny.

"Tonight we will. We need a closer look at the houses inside the property," said Kyle.

"Sweet! I'm in," said Kenny.

"Who else is in?" asked Fuentes.

"Not you. You have to stay and watch Suzy's back. Jesse stays too, so that he can continue to help Suzy get connected with the National Crime Information Center (NCIC)," said Kyle. Fuentes looked disappointed. "Aw! Look at that. I think he's gonna miss you, Kenny," said Kyle while making a baby face.

"Who can blame him?" said Kenny with pride.

"I can," said Suzy.

"You can have a glass of shut the hell up," said Kenny to Suzy.

"That was from the movie *Happy Gilmore*," said Kyle.

Kenny showed Suzy how the goggles worked with the computers and gave her a run-down on the commands. "Normally, I handle all the goggle commands. But you should know what you're doing by now," said Kenny. "Tonight will be a good test run for you."

"Are you saying I need to run?" asked Suzy with an insulted look on her face.

"How the hell did you get the impression that I was calling you fat from 'tonight will be a good test run'?" asked Kenny.

"I'm just getting your dander up, jeez," said Suzy.

"Plus, if I were talking about your weight..." said Kenny with Suzy watching closely, "I would have said you needed to sprint until passing out," said Kenny on the jog. Suzy caught him and punched him in the right arm repeatedly until he took it back.

"O.K., I take it back," yelled Kenny.

"I thought so, punk," said Suzy as she got off him. Kenny got up and walked over to Kyle.

"My arm stings. She was really putting some 'weight' into those punches," said Kenny. Kyle started laughing until they both saw Suzy coming with her taser out. Jesse never saw two men move so fast in such a short period of time.

Suzy now had five computers to monitor. "One for each pain-in-the-butt brother," she told James, "one for information sharing, one for security with camera links and one for games."

"Why the one with games?" asked Jesse.

"Are you kidding? You've been on boring stakeouts before, haven't you?" asked Suzy.

"I certainly have. But watching your brothers is far from a boring stakeout," said Jesse.

"Says you," said Suzy. "I've been watching them my whole life. There isn't much they can do now that would surprise me."

"Still. These video goggles are top notch. We're going to get to watch the whole thing," asked Jesse.

"We sort of have to. I control most of the goggles' functions from here. According to Kenny, I watch the terrain and give them what they need when they need it. It's a piece of cake," said Suzy.

"Yeah. It's gonna be a good movie," said Fuentes. Kenny and Kyle came out dressed in all black.

"What's going to be a good movie?" asked Kenny thinking he missed something.

"He was implying you two, but I assured him that there's really nothing to it," said Suzy. Jesse was noticing the gear on the two brothers. All black, lightweight and breathable with soft vests and soft leg armor.

"Before you ask, the guns are KR-7's. It's just a modified MP-5 with a few extras. Oh, and .357 rounds of course," said Kenny.

"With silencers and shoulder straps to boot? Nice," said Jesse.

"Thank you," said Kenny.

"Are those the ones you used on the victims?" asked Jesse. Kyle and Kenny turned to look at Jesse. Fuentes and Suzy looked away from the scene.

"Never ask us that again, Detective James. And when you say victims, you mean murderers, right?" asked Kyle.

A long silence in the room and James said, "Sorry about that."

"We're out of here. We're going to try an insert at the northwest corner of the property. Night vision first and we'll go from there," said Kyle.

"Gotcha," said Suzy.

As they were exiting the trailer Kenny turned to Jesse and said, "Chin up, little buckaroo. Watch the movie and enjoy. This is for you and your brother too."

Chapter 36

Kenny and Kyle took the Hummer to a nearby abandoned strip mall and parked in the back. "This way, little brother," said Kyle as he walked off towards the ranch property in a low crouch.

"Should we give them exciting banter while we do this or what?" asked Kenny.

"Keep your head in the game and not on entertaining the others," snapped Kyle. Then he thought about it for a second and said, "And, yeah, every now and then is cool. No reason to make it boring." Kenny smiled at this. He always thought Kyle needed to loosen up on the operations.

A message across their LED screens at the bottom of their goggles said, "It's already boring. Go shoot some dogs or something." Kenny flipped his own goggles the bird. Another message on the LED screen, "That's not nice, Kenny. Want me to try the new 50,000 watt attention getter I added to y'all's goggles this morning?" Kenny quickly took a knee and took off the goggles for a quick examination. Nothing new on the goggles.

"That wench. I'm gonna get her for messing with me," said Kenny.

"Can we at least get on the property before you two start?" asked Kyle.

"Made you look," said the LED screen crossing Kenny's goggles. Kenny gripped his KR-7 tighter as if he were choking Suzy and smiled.

They approached the northwest corner of the property and watched the fence line for movement. The dogs were still out there but it was too dark to get a bead on them. Even with the night vision goggles.

"Give me heat signatures, Suzy," said Kyle in a low whisper. Kyle's goggles went instantly black with the exception of three walking dogs shaded in red. Each was in its assigned area and was pacing the fence line. "How many dogs you want to put out?" asked Kyle just as he heard three short puffs of air from an air pistol.

"The three you were looking at are already napping," said Kenny.

"Did you see that?" asked Jesse. "Three dogs down in less than two seconds. All shot in the chest too, from what I could see. That was amazing," gasped Jesse. "We're going to kick some butt out there tonight." To which both Kenny and Kyle held up their thumbs to their goggles.

"It's fun watching, right?" Fuentes asked Jesse.

"It is when you're watching those two," said Jesse.

"Not so loud. If Kenny hears you he might start doing rollovers or cartwheels or something stupid," said Suzy. Just then a quick jerk of Kenny's goggles and he was watching movement from behind Kyle. Someone else was there and in all black. Suzy gave them back their night vision and alerted Kyle to watch his six. A quick burst on fully automatic into the area sent one man down. Kenny heard the sound of the man's weapon hit a tree trunk or something hard. The noise alarmed some more dogs down the property line and they came to check what might be an unsecured area.

"Great. More dogs," said Kyle. Kenny and Kyle took a knee together and waited for the dogs. By the time it finally got quiet, eight dogs had been put to sleep. And one man was permanently out of service.

"We haven't even crossed the fence yet," said Kenny.

"I know. This is ridiculous. Talk about paranoid. And what's with the ninja guy back there?" asked Kyle.

"Must be training for the rookies. 'Hang out in a tree tonight in sector 9JC. If anyone gets by you then I am going to take a personal interest in seeing you suffer,'" said Kenny in his best training sergeant's accent. "Hey. Stands to reason if there's one, there might be more," thought Kenny and Kyle must have been thinking the same.

"Heat signature, Suzy," said Kyle. They took a knee again and began searching the tree line outside the fence. There were four more men out there in similar positions as the first. "No need to kill these guys. They don't even now we're here," said Kyle.

"I'll put them to sleep. I don't want anyone else sneaking up on our six tonight," said Kenny.

"Fine. Put them to sleep," said Kyle knowing that Kenny just wanted to show off his shooting again. Though the man furthest from them was about fifty yards down, Kenny had them all tagged and out in less than two minutes. He even returned with a couple of wallets.

"Are you kidding me? Wallets? Who the hell teaches these people combat tactics? Macy's?" asked Kyle.

"Don't hate me because I'm beautiful," said Kenny. Kenny handed one wallet to Kyle and they both found picture identification on the ninjas wannabes. They both held the photo I.D.'s to their goggles for Suzy to get a snapshot of them and run them through NCIC.

"These guys are nobody special. Probably just as Kenny said, they're rookies doing their time on the fence line. And shut up, Kenny," said Suzy. Now that the outside cleaning was finished, the brothers examined the fence for trip wires. There were two trips. One on the bottom and one in the middle of the fence running horizontally. You have to snap it and reconnect it to your wire in less than a second or risk setting off the alarm. Your wire is the battery back-up so the line thinks it's still connected. Two quick snaps and the fence wires were done. Even Fuentes was impressed with the fence wire maneuvers. Kyle cut a hole in the fence with his bottle of metal cutter, because he was tired of waiting for Kenny to cut each individual link with his Rambo knife.

"Put that stupid knife up. Let's go," said Kyle.

"It worked in the movie," snapped Kenny.

There were five structures on the property according to the latest aerial photos. The two smaller structures to the far north of the property look like storage sheds for equipment. Kenny and Kyle were slowly approaching the largest of the three buildings, probably the barracks.

Chapter 37

"If they have look outs on the outside, it stands to reason that they have them on the inside, don't you think?" asked Kenny.

"Yeah. I've been looking around and I don't see any," said Kyle.

"If they're called lookouts on the outside, are they called lookins on the inside?" asked Kenny while slowly approaching the building.

"Good question. There is a trip wire at your feet," said Kyle to Kenny as calmly as if he were ordering a sandwich at Subway. Kenny looked down and saw the trip wire. It was connected to a double flare designed to illuminate the grounds and wake everyone from their slumber. Kenny wanted to make sure he remembered its location. It might come in handy.

"Mark this spot on the map, Suzy, for a double flare trip wire," said Kenny.

The LED response that Kenny read across his goggles was "Got it. Good thing Kyle is paying attention, huh?" Kenny was remembering how quiet it used to be on these assignments. Kyle had made it to the front of the building and was holding while Kenny was steady checking their six o'clock. Kenny had just finished his check when he noticed something unusual. A device that looked something like a motion detector hanging from the roof. Kenny froze for a second and asked Suzy to get a close up of it.

Suzy took a snapshot of it and after a quick look sent back, "It's a custom job. Can't even tell what it does."

"Kyle had already passed it, hadn't he?" thought Kenny. Kyle motioned Kenny forward. He must have been thinking the same thing. "Maybe it's inoperative," said Kenny and as he moved toward Kyle he heard a faint click and thought, "Shit!" Kyle watched as a large piece of the roof over Kenny's head became detached. It looked like it was about two feet by two feet square and was on a spring-loaded pulley of sorts. Kenny was almost out of its way when it hit him in his right side. He was able to shield his face and head, but the impact threw him in to the wall and his left side shattered a window. Kyle rushed over and pulled on the board that had Kenny pinned against the wall and a broken window. "Didn't see that coming," said Kenny with a raspy voice.

"Neither did I," said Kyle as he got enough slack out to free Kenny.

"It's gonna start raining men here pretty soon, brother," said Kenny. Just as Kenny finished his sentence, two men decided to stick their heads out of the broken window next to the Rhobertses. Kenny knocked the first one out with a single punch to the nose. "That's for that roof contraption," said Kenny. Kyle grabbed the second man and pulled him through the window as if pulling a rag doll from a crib. Kyle kept his right hand over the man's mouth while his left hand had a handful of hair. Kenny ran up to the man and taped his mouth shut. Kenny and Kyle started to move towards the hole in the fence that they had cut earlier.

While moving, Kenny was able to get a pair of flexi-cuffs around the man's hands to keep him from flailing about. Kenny also managed to convince the man that if he did not cooperate, he would be killed. A simple stare with a gun pointed at your face can convince a man to do many things. He definitely got the point. Kenny and Kyle made it to the fence and were crawling through it when they heard more dogs being released and the alarms going off. Kenny dropped some pepper mace grenades to mess with the dogs. It would make it harder for the dogs to track them. One of the dogs was too quick for the grenades and regrettably, Kenny had to put him down. Kyle watched as Kenny took a knee and held out his left arm for the dog. When the dog went to bite the left arm that was extended towards him, Kenny plunged his Rambo knife in to the dog's neck. Death was instantaneous. Kenny hated to kill dogs, but when he was not given a choice, there's not much to do about it. Kyle was impressed by Kenny's speed on the dog. The action against the dog sounds simple, but it's actually a very difficult move.

"Did you see that?" asked Jesse. "He took that dog out before I knew the dog was there."

"I saw that," said Fuentes.

"He's gonna be moody now, you watch," said Suzy.

"Why? That was a brilliant move," said Jesse.

"Kenny is overcritical of himself. The first thing he's going to contemplate is the roof top trap he discovered. The second, and more serious thing he is going to dissect, is the dog. Kenny loves dogs and it kills him to put them down. Still. Since I am his sister, I could lighten the load a little," said Suzy.

Kenny's LED screen flashed on in his goggles and read, "Dog-Killer!"

Kenny gave a brief smile and said, "*National Lampoon's Vacation.*" They made it back to the Hummer without incident and threw the hostage in the back.

"Now for a little questionnaire," thought Kyle.

Chapter 38

Kenny and Kyle were driving southbound on I-75 and watched several McKinney squad cars pass them going northbound with their lights and sirens on. "I wonder what they're up to?" asked Kenny.

"Probably just pissed off that someone broke in to their property and messed up their good night's sleep. I couldn't blame them. If someone broke in to my place, I'd probably hit the roof," said Kyle with a smile.

"I was totally waiting for that. Just wondering how you were going to relate it to something. Took you long enough," said Kenny.

"Well when one aims for the sky and all you do is hit the roof..." said Kyle smiling.

Kenny interrupted Kyle and said, "Shut it! They're just getting worse."

It was quiet in the Hummer for a minute until Kyle started humming, "The roof, the roof, the roof is on fire."

When they arrived at the trailer, they threw the hostage into a small metal storage shed and locked him in after hog tying him. The hostage was a Caucasian male, about thirty years old, five foot eight, 150 pounds, brown hair, brown eyes, short military-type hairdo and a very pronounced hair lip. He was wearing a white jumpsuit like you see prisoners wearing on the side of the road when they're cleaning. Kenny and Kyle went in to the main trailer to power down and take off their gear. "Jesse? How about you take the first run on this guy? Are you up to it?" asked Kyle.

"Are you kidding? I'd love to," said Jesse.

"Fuentes, go mask up and prepare two cameras in the shed. Take out the long table from inside the Hummer and set out the surgeon's instruments," said Kyle as he turned to look at Jesse and said, "It's just for effect."

"I hope not. This may be the only guy I can question about my brother's death, and believe me; the normal rules don't apply here. I've been dying to conduct an interview on my own terms," said Jesse.

"Let's concentrate on the group first, then when we have what we need, take all the time in the world getting your own answers," said Kenny.

"I'll try and stay on top of it," said Jesse with a grin.

"Good. I...oh, a roof joke. How original," said Kenny.

"Thank you," said Jesse.

"We'll go no rules in the interrogation room. When this guy breaks, and he will, let him spill out all of it before offering him any relief. Agreed?" asked Kyle.

"Agreed," said Jesse. Fuentes had his mask on and had set the two cameras up in the shed. He made a nice show of putting down plastic around the hostage and setting up the table with the scalpel and forceps and the rest of the tools. He never made eye contact with the hostage. "It gives them false hope," thought Fuentes. For an added bonus, Fuentes took a few older mattresses and tied them against the wall for sort of a sound barrier. Or he hoped the guy would believe it to be. Kenny, Kyle, Jesse and Suzy were already watching from the trailer where the lines from the cameras were directly fed. Fuentes looked like he was having fun messing with this guy's mind. They could see the panic in the hostage's face. He was sweating profusely and his jumpsuit was stuck to his body. Every time Fuentes passed him in the shed, the man made an attempt at eye contact with Fuentes, but Fuentes wasn't buying today. After about thirty minutes of prep time, Fuentes was finished and returned to the trailer.

"The man in that room may already be broken," said Fuentes. "Before I left the shed, he started whimpering. It shouldn't take you that long."

"Take them out of their environment and they're as harmless as a heels hound," said Kenny while putting his feet up on the counter to watch the show. "I got my popcorn ready and it's time for my favorite show, *Cops*."

"That's right. Do you have a strategy yet?" asked Kyle.

"I won't form my strategy until I've talked to him for a while," said Jesse.

"Of course," said Kyle a little too excited. He wanted to see just what Jesse was going to do this guy. He always wanted to watch an experienced detective interrogate a suspect. "Go get 'em, Tiger," said Kyle.

"*Spider-Man 2*," said Kenny. And that gave Detective James an idea. He asked Fuentes to take a large wooden basin and place it in the shed with the hostage.

"Fill it full of water so that if this guy harbors a fear of drowning, like most people do, I can use that too."

"That's fiendish! I love it, you sick bastard," said Kenny.

"I'll bet you've been dying to find a way to say 'fiendish' all day, haven't you?" asked Suzy.

"I like the word and rarely have an opportunity to use it. So when I choose to bless your ears with my intellectual verbage, do me a favor and savor the moment," said Kenny with his nose raised and a pompous look on his face. Suzy just rolled her eyes at Kenny. "Now be gone, servant. I shall call you when I need something," demanded Kenny. "And you," Kenny said to Detective James, "go and seek knowledge from our hostage, fledgling."

Chapter 39

The interview took Detective James every bit of six hours. Kenny and Kyle never stopped watching the interrogation. Kenny was very impressed with what James was able to accomplish. The tactics of Detective James surprised Kyle. He never thought James was capable of torture. He was wrong. Suzy did not watch the interviews. She just wanted to hear about the results. Fuentes watched from a distance and seemed impressed with James' tactics. "It's nice to watch from a different perspective," he thought. Detective James entered the trailer and plopped down into the La-Z-Boy. Kenny brought over a large glass of ice water and handed it to James.

"You did great, Jesse," said Kenny.

"Thanks. I am whooped. Think I'll get some shut-eye. Can you guys go over the tapes and..." said James.

"Already on it," interrupted Kyle.

"Thanks again," said Jesse.

"You did all the work, kid. We just watched the show," said Kyle.

Detective James was able to get a lot of information from the hostage. It appeared that the Rhoberts brothers snagged a good one on their first attempt. His name was not important, just the information. The group known as Armageddon was just what it seemed. A group of people who believed something so drastic, they were willing to wage a war over it and end all of humanity if it meant not getting things their way. They hadn't separated by race yet, but by the appearances of several different break-off sanctions, it was coming. They believed in stronger borders in the south and getting rid of all illegal aliens. They believed that if you are not born in the United States, then don't bother coming over to reap the benefits. Benefits paid for in their family's blood in war after war. "True Americans," as they put it, should get priority and benefit over all who are not. They didn't believe the word "American" was anyone who came over to the United States and worked for a living. They believed that if you were found crossing the border illegally, you should be shot. They believed that the punishment of any crime committed by an illegal alien must be treated more severely than by a "true American." They talked about overthrowing the United States government because it had no uses other than feeding the rich and screwing the poor. They believed video surveillance and enforcement of traffic laws by camera were unconstitutional.

"You can write a whole encyclopedia volume on what these turds believe and don't believe," said Kenny.

"What I fail to see is the connection between the Armageddon group and our parents," said Kyle.

"Maybe Dad is a 'true American.' Not like this guy," said Kenny as he pointed toward Fuentes.

"It gets me sometimes when people take the wrong stand on a decent subject. Some of the points they make are valid. It is the extremist attitude towards the conclusion of the problems that make them nuts, in my opinion," said Fuentes.

"Thank you, Doctor, for that insightful look into our hostage's mind. Join us next week when we go into the mind of a four-time divorcee who insists that hell is right here on earth," said Kenny holding his thumb up like a microphone.

"He has a point. I don't believe video surveillance and camera enforcement is right either," said Kyle.

"But you're not going to blow up a police station to prove your point, are you?" asked Kenny.

"No. But I would protest the ticket," said Kyle.

"That's my brother," said Kenny holding his hands out to Kyle. "Courtroom drama extraordinaire. What are you going to do? Tell the judge that if you knew the camera was there, you wouldn't have been speeding?" asked Kenny.

"No. I'll tell him that I have a right to speed if I want to. If I personally choose to break the law, then I must be willing to take the punishment if I'm caught," said Kyle.

"But let's say you were caught, on camera," said Kenny.

"No. I have to be caught by a person. An officer, not a freakin' camera," said Kyle.

"Ahah! You just don't like the fact that a camera is the new way of enforcement. Incidentally, you don't have a right to speed. You have a right to drive, but not to speed," said Kenny.

"I was simply making a point about freedom. Don't dissect it," said Kyle. "And it's more about the slow disillusionment of losing one's freedoms that concerns me. There are already too many cameras on streets today. Pretty soon, you won't be able to go anywhere off camera."

"I don't mind being on camera," said Kenny.

"That's because you're a show-off and you love yourself more than anybody," said Kyle.

"I just enjoy life is all. Jealousy rears its ugly head, again," said Kenny shaking his head at Kyle.

Chapter 40

"It's Shoemaker," said James when he sat up on the couch. "Why didn't it hit me in the room when he said it?"

"When he said what?" asked Kenny.

"The name 'Shoemaker.' It's on the tape in the second hour. He mentions the name of one of the decision-makers at the corporate level. He didn't exactly say he was in charge, but who cares. We already made the connection," said James.

"What connection?" asked Kyle.

"If John Shoemaker, Sr. was one of the top men of Armageddon, it would explain everything," said James.

"Why would it explain everything?" asked Kenny.

"Because Kenny and Kyle killed John Shoemaker, Jr. last week in Dallas. I worked the crime scene, remember? That carjacker you guys killed came back with a positive I.D. on John Shoemaker, Jr. Now, don't get me wrong. The guy deserved exactly what he got. But it explains the timeline, doesn't it?" asked James. "Follow me here. The hit is placed on Shoemaker, Jr. and Suzy accepts the hit on y'all's behalf. Someone with connections, like Suzy, finds out who owns the hit on Shoemaker, Jr. and tries to send a message to the contractor that he had better not honor the contract. I'm assuming Shoemaker, Sr. was trying to stop the contract or buy it out. That was when the heroin addict received orders to burn down your parents' home. He was supposed to be sending a message to you two," and Jesse motioned to a reluctant Kyle and Kenny, "that you guys needed to forget about the contract. However, he couldn't get the message to you before the deed was done. I'll bet you good money that someone knows about you two cleaning up the streets," as he motioned to Kenny and Kyle. "That they know about your dad's training and your family's background and experience. And they know you hit Shoemaker, Jr.," said Jesse pleased with himself.

"It certainly answers a lot of questions. Are you just spit-balling here or is this an honest to God detective's theory?" asked Kyle.

"It's the best I can come up with," said Jesse.

"Sounds pretty good to me," said Fuentes.

"It's got my vote. You can find out just about anything you want with enough money. And if Shoemaker, Sr. is part of the corporate crowd in the higher-ups of Armageddon, he would certainly have access to a lot of money," said Suzy.

"We'll go with it since it's the only connection we have," said Kyle.

"So what now?" asked Fuentes.

"We find Shoemaker, Sr. and convince him that his grudge against the Rhobertses is over," said Kenny.

"And some of their cronies over at the camp still need a few lessons in manners," said Kyle.

"We going back in?" asked Kenny.

"Hell, yeah! If we can get some more information about this group, it will be easier to find a weakness and tear them down," said Kyle.

"How deviant of you. Always scheming. I like it," said Kenny.

"You two do not need to go back in to that compound," said Suzy. "It's an unnecessary risk. All we have to do is find Shoemaker and finish this."

"It's true that our problems will be over after we take care of Shoemaker. But our country's problems still exist with this group and I don't like the idea of these guys out there," said Kyle. Kenny started humming the national anthem. Fuentes jumped up and gave a salute to Kenny as he hummed along with him. "Whether you turds realize it or not, we have an obligation to this country to help rid it of scum like this. We do it because we can and most people can't," said Kyle.

"I don't know why you feel that responsibility. I don't feel it," said Suzy.

"You don't feel at all, except for the bullfrogs, of course," said Kenny to Suzy, "You're like a de-gutted empty cold catfish. Just a money and mud grubber. A bottom feeder. You're the Rhoda," said Kenny smiling at Suzy.

"I am not the Rhoda," said Suzy, "And that little gem is from *Romy and Michelle's High School Reunion.*"

"Do I get to go this time?" asked Fuentes.

"Have you been a good boy?" asked Kenny.

"As good as can be expected around you two," said Fuentes to Kenny and Kyle.

"Oh, just let him go. Detective James can watch my back as I watch y'all's," said Suzy.

"If you go, you go last and stay behind Kenny," said Kyle.

"Understood," said Fuentes with a smile. He'd been waiting to show the brothers what he could do in a covert operation. Now was his chance.

Chapter 41

Kenny and Kyle led Fuentes to the northeast corner of the compound. They couldn't go in the same spot twice. That would be reckless. They were prepared this time for the outside resistance. Armageddon members didn't change their tactics; they just fortified them more. There were sixteen in the woods this time. All on the outside of the fence line in the trees. Kenny and Fuentes took care of fifteen of them and Kyle dropped one close to the fence where they made entry. "Get ready for the dogs," whispered Kenny to Fuentes.

"I can handle a few watch dogs," said Fuentes.

"Don't get cocky. I don't want the dogs hurt if it's possible. Just take them out with the darts I gave you," said Kenny with earnest.

"If you have to take one, do it quietly," whispered Kyle. Fuentes nodded that he heard what Kyle had said. "Let's move to the front building this time and watch for the traps. Kenny, that goes double for you," said Kyle. Kenny mumbled something under his breath but no one heard him. There were two McKinney police squads parked in the circular driveway in front of the main building. "Bingo. They will, no doubt, be protecting the records and the office areas," said Kyle.

"Let's go,' said Kenny. Just then, Kenny fired the first shot as he observed a sniper on the roof of the first building. The sniper put a bullet in Fuentes' left shoulder. Fuentes took a knee and gave the wound a quick peek.

"Just a scrape. Let's move," said Fuentes. Kenny came over to look at the wound and it had already bled down the arm to his hands.

"You are no good to us bleeding out. We cannot carry you if it hits the fan. I'm sorry, Sarge, but you just became a crutch and when the troops start to arrive, we need all our focus on them," said Kenny.

"Can you make it back to the Hummer?" asked Kyle.

"I can complete this mission, sirs," said Fuentes.

"There's a good lad. Just wanted you to have the opportunity to back out with pride," said Kenny. Kenny had no more finished his critique on Fuentes when another shot fired from the rooftops of the barracks building where they caught the first hostage. It was a miss but they had Fuentes in their targets again.

"Would you seek some kind of cover, please," said Kyle to Fuentes.

"Well if you two would stop talking," said Fuentes.

"Oh, I'm sorry. It's hard to hear with all these sniper rifles going off," said Kenny.

"Smartass," said Fuentes.

"Rookie,' said Kenny.

"We have to get inside the building. Kenny, take lead and find us a way in," said Kyle. "We'll cover the rooftops until you advise."

"I'm on it. Take notes, rookie," said Kenny to Fuentes. Kenny moved very fast at a run and hugged the building as he made his way around it looking for the best entry point. The north side had a double pane window and it was open. "Moving in," said Kenny, "Suzy, give me a body heat signature scan on the room I'm clearing." His goggles changed at once to infrared body heat and he observed three in the room crouched below the open window. "Time for one of my specialties," thought Kenny.

Kenny crouched below the window and tossed in a pepper ball grenade. A small pocket of compressed cotton that surrounded the grenade that Kenny designed to keep the noise to a minimum had muffled the sound of the grenade. Kenny did not wait for the grenade to go off before jumping in to the window and was caught by surprise. The three inside were wearing gas masks and were ready for his grenade. Kenny dropped two of the group in less than a second, but the third got Kenny in the back with what felt like a baseball bat or baton.

Kyle and Fuentes had made their way to the window and began to climb inside when reinforcements arrived in the room.

Kyle watched as a McKinney police officer, dressed in SWAT gear, was dragging off Kenny into another room. Fuentes grabbed Kyle before entering the room and said, "It's no good. They have more coming down the hallway and we are seriously outnumbered. Our flank is wide open and the entire compound is headed this way."

"They've got my brother, damnit," said Kyle.

"And they'll have us too if we don't get out of here," said Fuentes. Kyle hesitated for a moment until the snipers started taking aim at them again. It was everything they could do just to get away from the front building without being tagged. "We have to leave him for now and regroup," said Fuentes.

"Back to the Hummer. And kill everything that moves," said Kyle as he started into a low, crouched run. Suzy and James were in a panic. Never had one of her brothers been taken in any operation that Suzy could remember. "Make the call, Suzy. Make the call. We have no choice," said Kyle in a full sprint now to avoid the shots. "And abandon the trailer ASAP. Get rid of the hostage and clean the place. When we get back, I want you two ready to roll. And did you receive my order to make the call? Acknowledge me, damnit," yelled Kyle in to his microphone.

"I received and the call is being made," said Suzy.

"Who are we calling?" asked Fuentes.

"Back-up is all you need to know," said Kyle. "How did this get so screwed up so fast?" thought Kyle. "Suzy was right. This was an unnecessary risk and now they have Kenny. If they harm a hair on his head, I'm gonna burn them all. Consequences be damned," thought Kyle. To Kenny, Kyle looked back at the compound and whispered, "I'll be right back, bro, don't you worry."

Chapter 42

The first call was to Timothy Rhoberts, the oldest brother. He lived in Houston, Texas, and owned several local taverns in a suburb of Houston called Katy. He was just finishing a meeting with a health inspector on one of his properties when his pager went off. The pagers all the brothers and Suzy carried were for emergencies only. Tim checked his pager and it read, "Kenny is POW. Bravo location. Fully equipped. Expedite. Suzy." Tim walked the inspector out and told him he was sorry but the meeting was over. Tim called a friend at Houston Hobby Airport who flew a jet and told him he needed a favor. "I need quick transport to the Dallas area with some private equipment and no questions."

"How fast?" asked the pilot.

"Ten minutes ago. I'm already en route to the airport," said Tim.

"Will do! I'll file the flight plan and try to have the bird ready when you get here. Tim, can I ask what this is all about?" asked the pilot.

"Just a family emergency," said Tim. "What have the two misfits got themselves into this time?" thought Tim. "I hope Kenny is all right. I'll bet Kyle is pacing the shit out of someone's floor right now."

The second call went to Ritchie Rhoberts, the second oldest. If you have not guessed by now, there are four brothers and one sister in the Rhobertses' immediate family tree. All well trained and versed in the ways of the United States Special Forces. Tim's specialty was tactics, armory and explosives while Ritchie could shoot the wing off a fly at five hundred yards in high wind. Ritchie Rhoberts was a local golf pro and private tutor to some of the local police departments for their tactical sniper squads. He held a sniper school for the police about once a month. Right now, however, he was on the eleventh green in Nacogdoches, Texas, on their local golf course. Ritchie lived in Nacogdoches because, for the most part, it was a quiet college town. Ritchie's pager went off after he hit a beautiful straight shot about half way to the green on a par five.

"Figures," said Ritchie. He looked down and read the pager's message, "Kenny is POW. Bravo location. Fully equipped. Expedite. Suzy." Ritchie looked at his golf ball and thought about it for just a second, then turned, put the club back in his bag and drove the golf cart towards the parking lot. "Why do they always get in to something when I'm playing a two under or better game?" thought Ritchie. He drove back to his home, threw his equipment in his newly acquired black 2007 Chevrolet Z06 Corvette and headed at high speed to the Dallas area. Bravo location was located in Frisco, Texas, at one of the Rhobertses' safe houses. It's only about thirty minutes south of McKinney, Texas.

Timothy arrived two hours after his page at bravo location and Ritchie an hour after that. Suzy brought them up to speed on current events and made the introductions.

"What happened, Kyle? How'd they get Kenny?" asked Ritchie.

"Didn't Suzy just show you the tapes and bring you up to speed?" asked Kyle.

"What I mean is what you were doing there?" asked Ritchie.

"All you need to know, Ritchie, is that Kenny was behind it one hundred percent or he wouldn't have gone and you know that," said Kyle.

"The blame game doesn't really work for me so can we just get on with the plan? We have a plan, right?" asked Tim.

"Yeah, we have a plan. We have had two excursions in their compound in less than twenty-four hours and none of the authorities have been contacted. Other than the locals that they own. They obviously do not want the attention. That works in our favor. We're going to burn it to the ground and kill every last one of them," said Kyle. "If you have any problems with that, you can go now, because that's what's happening." Everyone knew not to argue with Kyle when he got this way.

"The colonel has provided us with the rest of my team. They will be here within the hour, fully equipped and ready to rock," said Fuentes.

"And does the colonel know the orders?" asked Kyle.

"Doesn't matter, Kyle. My men will follow me in to hell and back and no one will lose an ounce of sleep over it," said Fuentes.

"As long as they know that what happens here, stays here. If anyone is a security threat, they will have to die. Period," said Kyle.

"When did we become assassins?" asked Ritchie.

"When these guys tried to kill Mom and Dad, burned their house down and captured Kenny," said Kyle.

"Good enough for me. Just wanted to be the voice of reason for a second since no one was doing it," said Ritchie while checking his rifle.

"Oh, yeah. They shot Fuentes in the arm and they were trying to kill Kenny and me," said Kyle.

"Where are your aerial photos? I want a look at all the local towers in the area," said Ritchie.

"Suzy has them set up in the garage," said Kyle. Ritchie and Tim went in to the garage with everyone trailing them. It was time to form a plan and a strategy.

"I just want you to get me inside the property. You guys find Kenny and get him out while I prepare all the buildings for demolition. All I need is a couple of your guys to watch my back as I set the charges," said Tim to Fuentes.

"That can be easily arranged," said Fuentes.

Chapter 43

Kenny woke up in an all white room with a headache the size of Texas. He vaguely remembered a baton to the back and something to the head before it all went black. There was an obvious observation glass facing Kenny and he realized that he was probably being watched. Kenny looked around the room and took everything in. There were four speakers in the room. One at each of the four corners of the room and they were white. He was sitting in what looked like a restraint chair that you would lock a raving lunatic in. Straps and wires were all over the base of the chair and Kenny's head and neck were not yet restrained. A couple of sprinkler heads over him in the ceiling and that was it. They must have a molding door or he came through the observation glass. Kenny was finished looking the room over and put his chin on his chest and settled in for a nap until they felt disposed to talk.

"I hope that Kyle and Fuentes are O.K.," thought Kenny. Just then, the speakers came on in the room and started playing the song "Don't Worry, Be Happy."

"I hate that song. So this is how it's going to be," thought Kenny with a smile on his face. "Guess they think they're getting even for the whole Waco play list that the Feds made the Davidians listen to," thought Kenny. "It's not doing much for my headache, but it's better than having an enema I suppose."

"I found a cell tower just off the property facing the front of the compound. Any chance we might be going right down the middle?" asked Ritchie.

"I figure it's best to come from two different angles. Fuentes' group from the front entrance and our group from the northeast corner again. We'll give Tim time to set his charges, find Kenny and get the hell out of Dodge before they know what hit them," said Kyle.

"I understand we only have three main buildings and a couple of sheds. Is that correct?" asked Tim.

"Yes," said Kyle.

"I'll blow the sheds first to cause the initial panic and give you time to locate Kenny. After the sheds are blown, you can give yourself approximately ten minutes before I get the main three. Is that enough time?" asked Tim.

"If I can't locate Kenny in ten minutes in that building, he ain't in it," said Kyle. "Ritchie, take one of Fuentes' men and have him post below you for ground cover."

"That won't be necessary. But thank you," said Ritchie.

"This is no time for overconfidence or cockiness, Ritchie," said Kyle.

"I know that, Kyle," snapped Ritchie.

"I'll be watching Ritchie in the tower," said Suzy. Fuentes and James turned with a look of surprise on their faces. Suzy was dressed in all black fatigues and had her own equipment on.

"Well, who is going to control the operations center and the technology we're linked into?" asked Kyle.

"That would be us, son," said John Rhoberts as he walked in to the room with Barbara right next to him.

"Dad, no offense, but do you even know how all this new technology works?" asked Kyle.

"Who do you think helped Kenny design most of this stuff?" asked John.

"I don't know. I guess I just figured it was his geek factor going wild," said Kyle.

"Well, rest assured, I can handle any of this equipment and your mother is going to be watching my back while I watch y'all's," said John.

"You didn't think we were going to sit this one out? Did you?" asked Barbara Rhoberts. "They have my son, and your brother. One thing you never do to a Rhoberts is insult the family or attempt to bring harm to it. You will lose," said Barbara Rhoberts with the most intense look on her face.

"This family is scary," whispered James to Fuentes.

"You have no idea," said Fuentes.

"No more discussions on who does what. When the rest of Fuentes' team gets here, we fill them in on the operational plan and go," said John Rhoberts.

"Suzy and I need to go now," said Ritchie. "I need to have time to climb and prep the area for escape if things get sticky. Two or three zip lines leading off the tower should be sufficient. Call us on the goggles when you guys are on approach."

"Will do. Be careful, Ritchie. Be careful, Suzy," said John Rhoberts.

"You two come back safe and bring me my Kenny," said Barbara Rhoberts with a swell of tears in her eyes.

Chapter 44

Two men entered the white room and Kenny feigned sleep. They each brought a chair in with them and they looked much more comfortable than the one Kenny was in. The two men were wearing black masks and fatigues. Everything was covered except for the eyes. Kenny looked up at them when they sat in front of him. He could tell that both men were Caucasian. "What are you doing here?" asked the first who was sitting on Kenny's right. Kenny looked down and gave no more eye contact nor did he respond to the question.

"What's your name? Now, there's no harm in giving us that, is there?" asked the second. Kenny continued to stare at the floor and began counting the variations in the floor.

"Lose yourself in thought. Especially if this gets ugly," thought Kenny.

"Fine! Let's hit him with some juice and see if he feels like talking," said the first as they both got up and backed away from Kenny. A strong current of electricity entered the chair and Kenny felt his body go stiff. It was probably just a five-second burst, like they gave

Detective James, but it felt like an hour to Kenny. When the burst was over, Kenny bit his tongue, let the blood spill out over his chin and faked an unconscious spell. "Check his pulse," said the first.

"He's fine. Just passed out," said the second.

"You used too much juice on him, genius. Now we have to wait for him to wake up again," said the first to whoever was behind the glass.

"What a bunch of morons," thought Kenny. "They don't know how to wake an unconscious? Works for me, though. I was just buying time here in the first place. Getting hungry though. This would make a good Snickers commercial. I'll have to remember to tell Kyle about this one. Being tortured? Not going anywhere for a while?" Kenny thought.

"Ritchie? Are you set?" asked Suzy.

"I'm good, Suzy. Find yourself a hole and watch my escape routes," said Ritchie.

"I've already got a spot picked out. I'll be at your six thirty in a creek side drain," said Suzy.

"I see it. That's perfect. I already have multiple targets," said Ritchie while looking through his scope.

"Not yet, Ritchie," said Suzy.

"I know. I know," said Ritchie. "Wait. Just let me get three of them. There is nowhere for those three to go and no one can trace them back to us." As Suzy started to answer Ritchie, she heard three consecutive silenced shots. "Three targets down. No one is the wiser," said Ritchie with a smile.

"O.K., you've had your fun. Now let's dig in until the troops arrive," said Suzy. Ritchie lowered his weapon and covered the scope. He pulled a black camouflage tarp over him that made his immediate area look like a power converter. Suzy heard Ritchie slow down his breathing and ease into a more relaxed state of mind.

"Let me know, Suzy," said Ritchie.

"I will. Sweet dreams," said Suzy shaking her head at her brother. Ritchie was the only one in the family that could sleep when he wanted and where he wanted. He could sleep on a hard rock in one-hundred-degree heat if he wanted. Suzy envied him for that. Not just the way he could fall asleep, but the way he just took out three other snipers in less than three seconds, reduced his breathing and was now taking a nap.

Fuentes team arrived with extra equipment and one extra soldier. "Colonel? What are you doing here?" asked Fuentes.

"Well, that's obvious, isn't it," asked the colonel.

"Sheldon?" said John Rhoberts. "You don't have to get mixed up in this."

"You know better than that, John. Those are my boys too. Besides, you think I'm going to let these kids have all the fun?" asked Colonel Smith.

"Well, we're certainly glad to have you," said Barbara Rhoberts.

"Maybe we can find a way to make this unofficially official," said Colonel Smith.

"Do you think that's possible?" asked John Rhoberts.

"It's all possible, John. We've seen it," said Colonel Smith.

"If you can convince the government that this group is a clear and present danger to the security of the United States," asked Fuentes.

"Yes, well we have all seen that movie, haven't we? Sarge, I think you took it a little too seriously," said Kyle.

"Let me guess," said Detective James. "*Clear and Present Danger?*"

"How do you do it?" asked Kyle.

"I'm in awe," said Fuentes.

"As well you should be. Fuentes, get your team up to specs. We move out in ten minutes," said Kyle. Tim was given two of Fuentes' men. One man for carrying the ordinance, and the other to watch their backs as they set them.

"We're going. I'll see you two at the rendezvous point in about twenty to thirty minutes," said Tim to Kyle and Fuentes.

"Good luck, bro," said Kyle. "Sorry about calling you guys out for this one."

"Are you kidding? I haven't blown anything up in over a month and I have a lot of stress to get rid of," said Tim with a smile.

Chapter 45

"We're here," said Kyle over the low-frequency microphone. "Operation is a go! Now! Now! Now!" said Kyle.

"That's the go code, Ritchie. Happy shooting," said Suzy. Kyle and Fuentes made a straight line for the building that Kenny had been subdued in. Fuentes told the rest of his team to concentrate on the other two buildings (and to stay clear of the sheds). Kyle and Fuentes just made entry into the same window Kenny was taken and heard the first explosion.

"One of the sheds must be littered all over the place," said Fuentes.

"You think?" whispered Kyle as he pulled a drill bit out of the wall in front of him.

"Well, Tim is certainly having a good time," said Ritchie to Suzy as he kept sniping people from his tower. "That's eighteen so far. I might go for Rambo numbers here," said Ritchie. "This almost makes me feel bad. These people haven't the slightest idea what they are doing. They're not even seeking cover from my fire."

"Serves them right for hooking up with the wrong people. Stupid is as stupid does," said Suzy.

"*Forrest Gump*," said Ritchie as he shot number twenty through the base of the skull. Another explosion in the second shed sent debris all over the grounds. This time, however, the shed was filled with ammunition.

"It's like the Fourth of July out there," said Fuentes.

"And if I know Tim, he's just getting started," said Kyle with a sly squint in his eye. As he finished speaking to Fuentes, a soldier dropped from the ceiling through the floor above. Fuentes and Kyle took a good look at him and he had been shot through the head by a sniper.

"That's a pretty good shot there, Ritchie," said Fuentes.

"Well, thank you, sir. How about this one?" asked Ritchie and the lights in the building occupied by Fuentes and Kyle went out.

"Very nice," said Fuentes.

"Night vision, Dad," said Kyle. And it was done before he could complete his sentence. Fuentes' team and the colonel must have cleared the main building because that was the next building to blow. And blow up it did.

"You'll pay particular notice to the accelerant I put in the fire. That building will be in ashes in five minutes," said Tim, "But as a plus, provides you with plenty of light for your job, Ritchie."

"You are too kind, Tim. How much do you want?" asked Ritchie as he hit numbers twenty-four and twenty-five.

"No charge for family," said Tim.

"Could I make a small request?" asked Ritchie.

"Feel free," said Tim.

"You remember the pine cones we used to burn on Christmas that turned different colors? That would have been a nice touch," said Ritchie.

"Well, then. My next compound accelerant fire will have more color. Just for you," said Tim, "Now if you'll excuse me. I have the grand finale to plan."

"That should be good," said Suzy as she shot an approaching soldier who was trying to flank them on foot. "Nothing better than a

Smith and Wesson .357 six inch revolver for those dumb ones that just start walking up while looking at the sky."

"Honestly. They concentrate too much on me and assume I won't have cover," said Ritchie.

"Well, you have killed twenty-eight of their friends," said Suzy.

"Twenty-nine," said Ritchie as he shot one at Suzy's six o'clock.

"Thank you, brother," said Suzy.

"Not a problem," said Ritchie.

Kenny was listening to what he thought was World War III. He knew what was happening by the sounds. Explosions and people dropping like flies all over the place. His brothers were here. "These people are so dead," thought Kenny. The two soldiers came back in to the room and grabbed Kenny forgetting that he was secure to the chair.

"Damn it. We don't have time for all of this," said the first in a panic.

Kenny spoke for the first time and said, "You're right. You two do not have much time at all. The best thing you can do is leave. Now." However, it was too late. As Kenny finished his sentence, the two were dropped in the doorway by gunfire and two figures emerged in the doorway. "Took you guys long enough," said Kenny.

"Did you wet your pants? Is that poo I smell in here?" asked Kyle.

"I missed you too. Did you call in the brothers?" asked Kenny.

"Well, of course. Doesn't anyone ever matter as much as the brothers?" asked Kyle.

"No they don't. Wives come and go. That's the plain truth of it," said Kenny with a huge smile on his face.

"O.K., what did I miss?" asked Fuentes.

"*Wyatt Earp*," said Kyle.

"That is one of the single most awesome lines ever said in a movie," said Kenny. "Learn it well, my son, for someday it will guard your life."

"Those are a mixture of movie lines and metaphors. You must be hungry or something," said Kyle to Kenny.

"You should ask me about my new Snickers commercial," said Kenny.

"What about the new Snickers commercial?" asked Fuentes while untying Kenny.

"I'll tell ya later," said Kenny.

Chapter 46

Kyle handed Kenny an MP-5 semi-auto and said, "Try and stay close this time."

"This isn't my weapon," said Kenny when they climbed out the back window.

"I didn't have a chance to search all of Ritchie's victims. And there are no pieces left of Tim's victims. So excuse the hell out of me," said Kyle. "We have Kenny, and apart from being himself, he's O.K.," said Kyle to the others over the microphone.

"Can we get of here now before it starts raining police?" asked Ritchie.

"Let's all head to the rendezvous point," said Kyle as a massive explosion took out the building they just occupied.

"Watch the trail, Ritchie," said Tim, and Ritchie was watching a trail of gunpowder leave the building that had just exploded and headed off in the opposite direction towards the training grounds. The gunpowder was burning a design into the landscape. Ritchie finally made it out just before it flashed bright white.

"That was a really nice touch, Tim. Congratulations on that one," said Ritchie.

"I wish everyone could have seen it," said Tim pretending to get teary eyed.

"Me too," said Suzy, "And when did we add lightning to our capital 'R' with a circle around it?" she asked.

"Just making a point, Suzy. This is what you get when you mess...you know," said Tim as he was trailing two of Fuentes' men to the rendezvous point. Fuentes' team members that were covering Tim were outstanding. Both of them didn't hesitate once and they even helped with placing some of the ordinance. "Colonel Smith and Sergeant Fuentes? These people you brought in with you were good. I would work with them anytime. Thanks for the help," said Tim.

"I'm glad you weren't disappointed, Tim. I'll pass it on," said Colonel Smith.

"Just how many people do you require to get me out of jail, brother?" asked Kenny as they ran alongside each other headed for the northwest corner of the woods.

"You're the baby of the bunch. Mom and Dad wouldn't have it any other way," said Kyle.

"Tell me you didn't drag Mom and Dad out here?" said Kenny.

"Who do you think is running your outfit's technology base, mister?" read an LED message running across Kenny's goggles.

"Dad! Cool! Is Mom there?" said Kenny.

"Yeah. She's here and very pleased to know that you and your brothers and sister are safe," read the next LED message.

"Could you tell Mom that I'm hungry?" Kenny said with a smile and Fuentes and Kyle began to laugh.

"She says that since you guys are still out, pick something up and she will let you pay for it for being so careless in being captured," read the LED message running across all of their goggles.

"Is there any word on John Shoemaker, Sr.?" asked Kyle to anyone.

"I doubt very seriously he would be here after the times we've hit this place," said Kenny.

"Then we have one more loose end," said Colonel Smith.

"It would seem so," said Kyle.

"I've got a pretty good idea where to start," said the colonel.

Back at the safe house in Frisco the entire group was having a meeting about how to get closure. "Shoemaker is the only one left and it ends, right?" asked Suzy.

"I think that depends on Detective James. Are we after your brother's killer or the group in general?" asked Kenny to Detective James.

"Are you guys kidding? I couldn't have done anything if it wasn't for y'all in the first place," said James.

"I think the question is, will you be satisfied when we finish John Shoemaker, Sr. or is there something else you require?" asked Fuentes.

"I don't need anything other than what we've already done. I feel like I already have closure, for my part. And thank you all for the help," said a very grateful Detective James.

"Good. Shoemaker is the last," said Ritchie.

"Until we get another job," said Suzy.

"I don't want to hear about it, Suzy," said Tim.

"You won't," said Suzy.

"Then about Shoemaker, who wants to know where he is and what he's doing?" asked the colonel.

"OH! I do! I do," said Kenny with his hand raised high in the air.

Chapter 47

John Shoemaker, Sr. couldn't believe what he was seeing on the monitors. The entire McKinney compound was in flames with only a few survivors. He had watched the monitors from his high-rise office/condo in Dallas. The entire compound was covered in digital technology. Cameras were located in the trees, grass, bushes, fences, buildings and nearby towers. Each camera was numbered and listed on a map on the main monitor. If you wanted to see the camera angle, you simply put the cursor on the camera in the map and clicked it. It was that simple. Nevertheless, nothing was simple about what John Shoemaker had just seen. An entire section of Armageddon, his life's work, had just been slaughtered. What was worse was that he was fairly sure that the U.S. military was involved.

"That was a tactical team following the demolitions expert," said Shoemaker to himself. "But were they police, military or mercenaries? The list of our enemies seems to keep growing and growing. However, so does the list of our allies. Becky?" said Shoemaker.

"Yes, Mr. Shoemaker," said Becky, his administrative assistant.

"Get General Spokes on the line for me and tell him it's urgent."

"Right away, Mr. Shoemaker," said Becky.

"Marking the training grounds with a large 'R'? They're not even trying to hide the fact that they were responsible for this. And responsible for the death of my son. Well, if it's a war you want, you can certainly have it."

"Mr. Shoemaker, General Spokes on line one for you, sir," said Becky over the intercom.

"Thank you, Becky," replied a now upset John Shoemaker, Sr. "General Spokes, John Shoemaker here. I need to discuss a problem that has just come to my attention and should be brought to yours."

"John Shoemaker, Sr. is sitting in his high-rise office and watching the reruns of what happened to his compound and followers," said the colonel. "He's also trying to ascertain whether or not the military was involved. Oh, he already knows that you two were there," pointing at Kenny and Kyle. "Now he probably suspects you were all there after Tim left your calling card."

"Why would he think the military is involved, Colonel?" asked Kyle.

"Because your mom and dad didn't have more than five kids and more than five hit that compound today. Shoemaker is not stupid. You don't get that rich and powerful by being stupid. Watch the tape long enough and you can pick apart any operation," said the colonel.

"Pick it apart how?" asked Kenny as if insulted.

"Pick it apart like find out how many you were? Where did you approach and where did you exit? How good were you and did you have any experience or training?" said the colonel. "You know, try and find a weakness."

"And are we concerned about his interest in the military ties?" asked Kyle.

"Not at all. I have myself, Sergeant Fuentes and his team on special assignment for training. No one will miss us for a week," said the colonel as his pager went off that was hooked to his belt. Kenny started laughing right away and it took the rest of them every ounce of restraint not to follow. "It's General Spokes. That's odd. I have not spoken to General Charlie Spokes in years. I have to make this call," said the colonel.

"Timing is a little coincidental, don't you think?" said Kyle to Suzy, who had difficulty hearing him because Kenny was still laughing.

"Too coincidental. I'll check out General Spokes and see what I can dig up," said Suzy as she walked out of the room.

The colonel returned to the room wearing an odd expression. "What's going on, Colonel?" asked Fuentes.

"General Spokes has been named our new company commander, effective immediately. He wants us to return to base so he can assess our training records and operations over the last month," said the colonel.

"He knows," said Suzy, "and I'll bet you anything he's dirty."

"What makes you say that? What did you find out?" asked Kenny.

"General Spokes is a multi-millionaire with holdings in Swiss banks, German banks and believe it or not, Mexican banks," said Suzy. "There is no way he accrued the amounts of money he has legally. The timing is too close to be considered merely a coincidence and most importantly, the phone number the general called you from has recently been called by none other than John Shoemaker, Sr.," said Suzy with a large grin on her face. She was very proud when she was able to leave a room for five minutes and come back with so much information.

"I can handle the general. He won't be a problem," said the colonel. "As for you guys," said the colonel to Fuentes and his team, "we have to report to base." The colonel asked Suzy, "Can you make me a copy of all that you just told us with account numbers and phone records?"

"Not a problem, Colonel," said Suzy.

"So, it's blackmail then?" asked Kyle.

"Oldest trick in the book and works like a charm when your adversary has political ambitions," said the colonel with a smile.

"Go ahead, Colonel," said Fuentes, proud that the colonel was showing some cojones.

"I'm not without skills," said the colonel.

"Hey, Colonel, can I ask you something?" asked Kenny.

"As long as it's not sarcastic," said the colonel.

"Not at all, Colonel," said Kenny with a serious look on his face. "I was just wondering if anyone has ever asked you, where were you when Colonel Sanders died?"

Suzy was not expecting that and blew Coca Cola through her nose as she laughed. "Kenny never learns," thought Suzy.

Kenny laughed at Suzy's misfortune and Kyle said, "Don't encourage him, Suzy."

Chapter 48

The colonel was the first back on base and he went straight to the general's new office. "Colonel Smith to see General Spokes, ma'am," said the colonel to the general's receptionist.

"Have a seat, Colonel. He'll be with you in a minute," said the receptionist.

"I don't think so," said the colonel and he walked by the receptionist and straight in to General Spokes' office. "Hey, Charlie," said Colonel Smith.

"Sheldon?" said the general. "What the hell are you doing barging in to my office like this?"

"I'm about to set a few things straight," said the colonel. "And I would dispense with the attitude for now because you're facing some serious problems." Sergeant Fuentes entered the room and set up a laptop computer terminal with a wireless satellite internet connection.

"What the hell is going on here, Sheldon?" asked the general.

"With you in a second, General," said the colonel. The colonel leaned in close to Fuentes and whispered, "Are we ready?"

"Yes, sir. We're on line and connected to Suzy's laptop. She has quite a presentation ready," said Fuentes.

"Excellent," said the colonel.

"Damn it, Sheldon, you had better start making some sense out of this insubordinate behavior," said General Spokes.

"General Spokes. You have been a very bad general. You have broken just about every code of honor we believe in and swore to protect. Your bank accounts are very impressive, General." And the colonel tossed copies of all of the general's accounts and the activity from them over the last five years. "And your friends are impressive too, but that is about to change." The general turned white as a ghost. He thought he had been so careful and cautious with the money and accounts. "I think it's safe to say that I could not only end your career right now, I could easily hand this over to the right people and you would be facing time in federal prison," said the colonel.

"What's the alternative?" asked the general.

"I'm so glad you asked, Charlie. You are going to cut all ties with John Shoemaker and his group Armageddon. I want everything you have on Shoemaker and all the other leaders of their group," said the colonel.

"I can't do that, Sheldon. Do you know who these people are?" asked the general.

"Yeah, I know." And the colonel motioned to Sergeant Fuentes and said, "We just got through kicking their asses."

"You had help, though," said the general.

"Maybe. But that's not the point," said the colonel. "The point is this. You can assist us in the capture of John Shoemaker or be dishonorably discharged from the United States Army, prosecuted for your crimes and god knows what would happen to a snotty-nosed general in the penitentiary. Oh, yeah. We're taking some of your money, too," said the colonel.

"Just how much are you planning on taking?" asked the general as he sat up in his chair.

"Ten million, unless you continue to piss me off," said the colonel. "You have over twenty seven million, so I would be happy if I were you."

The general looked exhausted. He leaned back in his chair and took a few deep breaths. It seemed to calm him. "I've been under Shoemaker's boot for some time now. If you take him, he has to die," said the general.

"Along with the others who are taking the laws into their own hands," said the colonel.

"That's pretty hypocritical. The Rhoberts family, whom I know you know, kills for money and power. How do you explain their actions?" asked the general.

"Speaking of the Rhobertses, General, that was your other alternative," said the colonel, and as he did, a laser sight was shining on the general's chest. Now another was shining in the general's left eye and made its way to his forehead. "And I don't feel the need to explain anything about the Rhobertses to you, Charlie. You should be very grateful," said the colonel.

"Oh, I'm grateful, Sheldon. Let's just see if you want what you're getting yourself into," said the general.

"We, General. What 'we' are getting ourselves into," reminded the colonel.

Chapter 49

It took a few payouts, but Suzy was able to get the blueprints of the high-rise office building that was occupied by John Shoemaker, Sr. All possible entry and exits were studied and memorized. "Is this going to be a snatch and grab or an interrogation or what?" asked Kenny.

"We'll play it as it goes. How's that?" said Kyle.

"I'd be doing a lot better if you would hurry up. I would have gotten us there by now," said Kenny as he was lying still in the air duct.

"I still think this air duct thing is lame," said Kyle.

"We're just using it to get close to his front door. I plan on walking right in the front door," said Kenny. "That is, if we ever get out of this air duct."

"I'm working on it, Mr. First-to-show-inappropriate-anger-on-Mars," said Kyle.

"A space movie with that comedian in it. I don't remember the title," said Kenny.

"You mean I stumped the master?" asked Kyle.

"Don't get used to it," said Kenny.

Kyle made his final cut on the wires that secured the main filter grate to the twentieth floor. The grate fell hard towards the tile floor and Kyle jumped out to catch it. Kenny grabbed Kyle's feet just in time and anchored his legs in the air duct. "Don't have very long," said Kenny with a note of urgency.

Kyle set the grate down and Kenny let him down just before falling through the opening. Kenny made a muffled sound when he hit the floor. He got up quick and was staring at Kyle who was biting his lip so he wouldn't laugh. "I don't even want to see you smile," said Kenny.

"This is me, not smiling," as Kyle pointed to his face.

"Can we go now? Or would you like to make another clumsy mistake?" asked Kenny.

"We can go now. Hey, Kenny? Have you ever fallen in love?" asked Kyle.

"Hardy, har, har. Very funny. Took you long enough," said Kenny.

John Shoemaker was surprised not to hear back from the general sooner and started to get a little nervous. Since he didn't entirely trust the general, he called in his own security force to keep him company. Four ex-Navy SEALs who were dishonorably discharged for excessive force were guarding him. They were good and John Shoemaker used them as trainers at some of the other camps. He had many complaints from the recruits in the beginning of training, but that was to be expected. The SEALs liked to put everyone through hell week, just like they went through. Helped them weed out the weak ones. It was the first week of training for the recruits and a real test of your strength, both emotionally and physically.

Two of them guarded the front entryway while the others were guarding the back door that led to the staircase. Shoemaker started pacing the floor in the living area and began to think aloud, "If I were going to attack this place, how could I do it without detection?" asked

Shoemaker to no one in particular. A beeping sound started and the ex-SEALs jumped up to investigate. It was coming from outside the building. Shoemaker was trying to help find the source of the noise when he saw it. A glob of gray putty stuck to the top of a three-paned window with a small blinking red light.

"Oh shit," said Shoemaker and the glass shattered and flew away from the building. The wind picked up instantly in the room and Shoemaker threw himself to the floor in anticipation of World War III. The SEALs were still brushing glass off themselves when they turned to see two figures in the front doorway. Both men in the doorway were wearing all black and already had their laser sights on the other men.

"Drop the weapons and go. This is not your fight," said Kyle. One of the men hesitated and Kenny shot him in the head with a quick burst of three. He fell to floor instantly and a pool of dark red blood began to stain the marble tile. "Last warning," said Kyle as he raised his weapon. The other three thought better of challenging the brothers after seeing their teammate's head blown open. The weapons were dropped and the SEALs double-timed it out the back door and down the staircase. "Now. What shall we talk about?" asked Kyle to John Shoemaker, Sr.

"*Raiders of the Lost Ark*," said Kenny. Shoemaker looked at Kenny and was confused by his statement. "Shut up," said Kenny to Shoemaker.

Chapter 50

"What do you two want from me? Haven't you taken enough?" said an emotional Shoemaker.

"We were just doing the job. Your son died a long time ago when you failed to teach him about right and wrong. His death is on your hands, not ours. Oh, and the death of the mother he shot in the back," said Kyle.

"And the kids that will grow up having seen their mother killed. The numerous other victims caused by your inadequate parenting that inevitably changed so many lives. It's all on you," said Kenny, while he and Kyle slowly approached Shoemaker.

"What are you going to do?" asked Shoemaker as he was slowly walking backwards.

"We're going to make sure it never happens again. At least by you and your kind. Your group is coming to an end, Shoemaker," said Kyle.

"Before you leave us, I'll need you to tell me all about who, what, when and where of the rest of your Armageddon camps," said Kenny.

"What guarantee do I have that you will let me live if I provide you with that information?" asked Shoemaker.

"Oh, you're not going to live. It's how fast you want to go. A bullet? Some broken bones? Acid on the body to slowly eat away the flesh? The possibilities are limitless," said Kyle.

"I hate the acid one. The smell is worse than burnt popcorn. Don't you hate that smell?" asked Kenny to Shoemaker who looked more confused than ever.

"Well yes, I do," said Shoemaker.

"Shut up," said Kenny.

"If you're not going to let me live then I'll take my secrets to the grave and give you two one of these," said Shoemaker as he showed his middle finger to the brothers.

"Not very nice," said Kenny.

Kyle grabbed Shoemaker's middle finger, slipped a cigar clipper over it and snapped it off. Kenny stuffed a rag into Shoemaker's mouth just in time.

"A little warning next time," said Kenny.

"Let's call in the crew," said Kyle with a smile.

"By all means, sir, call away," said Kenny.

Kyle got on his cell phone and simply said, "Come on up. We're ready." He closed his cell phone and looked at Kenny. "They're on their way."

"Now you've done it," said Kenny to Shoemaker.

Detective James entered the room to find one body already on the ground and John Shoemaker, Sr. on the floor holding his right hand tightly with his left and blood was pouring down his arm. A large rag was stuffed in his mouth and he was trying to plea for his life. "You guys don't waste any time," said James. Looking at Shoemaker, Sr. now, "My name is Jesse James," said Detective James with his right hand extended to John Shoemaker. "Oh. I see you cannot shake hands. Pity. Let me introduce an associate of mine, Detective Drew Michaels. He is with our Crime Scene Division." As if on cue, Detective Drew Michaels entered the room and looked around with excitement. He was carrying two large briefcases and was inadvertently staring at the Rhobertses. "Drew? The crime scene," reminded Detective James.

"Oh, yeah, I'm on it," said Detective Michaels.

Drew Michaels carefully left evidence inside Shoemaker's office that implicated General Spokes and Shoemaker in several unsolved crimes in the Dallas, Texas area. Michaels left a few of the marble cameras, some receipts from ammunition specialists, a used KR-7 that matched ballistics from several crime scenes in Dallas and a love letter from Shoemaker to General Spokes with details from their last encounter (Kenny's idea). Kyle winked at James and said, "I told you earlier that you would get your bad guys." The icing on the cake was a life insurance policy that Suzy had doctored. Shoemaker, Sr. purchased a million-dollar life insurance policy for Shoemaker, Jr. Then, in an odd turn of events, Shoemaker, Sr. had something to do with a contract on his own son.

"This is going to make it to one of those *CourtTV* shows, I just know it," said Kenny while Michaels was placing the documents on Shoemaker's desk.

"If you two are detectives then protect me from these two lunatics," mumbled Shoemaker. Detective James approached Shoemaker and removed the rag in his mouth.

"They are recently retired. They found a better offer," said Kyle.

"With dental," said Kenny.

There was a pause for effect because of Kenny's last statement. "Did you know a Frank James, Mr. Shoemaker?" asked Detective James.

"Who?" asked Shoemaker who was pretending to choke a little from the rag.

"Frank James," said Detective James as he was putting on some thick leather gloves.

"Never heard of him," said Shoemaker.

"Wrong answer," said James and he hit Shoemaker square in the nose with his right fist. It broke immediately and blood began pouring from the cut on the bridge. Detective Michaels was setting up a table with surgical instruments and taking great care in their placement. John Shoemaker sat back up and spit a large glob of blood at the floor.

"O.K., the information you want is in my safe. The safe is in the bathroom behind the mirror and the combination is left six, right six, left six," said Shoemaker.

"Beware the numbers, 666," said Kenny.

"Very well," said Kyle to Shoemaker when he made his way to the bathroom. Kyle came back with files on six different campsites that had compounds just like the one they destroyed. Kyle motioned to Detective James and gave him thumbs-up.

Detective James grabbed his service revolver from his holster, a Smith and Wesson model 686, .357 and walked up to John Shoemaker and said, "Rest in peace, Frank," and he pulled the trigger.

A long few minutes passed in the room until Kenny asked, "You O.K., Jesse?"

"Yeah. I'm good. I'm real good. Thanks Kenny," and with a nod to Kyle, "Thank you, Kyle."

"Anytime, bud," said Kyle.

Kenny took the files from Kyle and began perusing them. "Looks like we have a lot of work to do," said Kenny.

"And we sure could use a cleaner," said Kyle to Detective Michaels.

"I'm in, if the money is good. I already enjoy the work. Setting up those two jerks was a pleasure," said Michaels.

"Money won't be a problem," said Kenny. "We don't really have dental or vision so you might want a day or two to think about it."

"No, I've been waiting my whole life for this," said Detective Michaels.

"Welcome aboard," said Kyle.

Kenny went over to Shoemaker's body and said, "Run, you cur, you tell them I'm coming, and Hell is coming with me, you hear, Hell is coming with me."

"*Tombstone*," said Detective James.

"That's my boy," said Kyle.

Drew Michaels stood confused for a moment and said, "Are you guys serious?"

"Always," said Kyle.

"Never," said Kenny.

THE END

Printed in the United States
68138LVS00002B/58-75